REVENGE OF THE ULTRAS

THE LAST HERO, BOOK 4

MATT BLAKE

MATTBLAKEAUTHOR.COM

If you want to be notified when Matt Blake's next novel is released, please sign up to his mailing list.

http://mattblakeauthor.com/newsletter

Your email address will never be shared and you can unsubscribe at any time.

M iami, Florida

ANNABELLE RICHARDSON DASHED down the sidewalk, eager
not to be late for her date.

The Miami sun was scorching. It was midday, so tourists
were out in their droves. Annabelle loved living in Florida. She
liked the heat; she liked the buzz of the place. She liked her trips
to the Keys to visit family. She liked pretty much everything
about it, except the tourists.

And yeah. There was a hell of a lot of tourists at this time of
year, in the middle of July.

She ran further down the sidewalk, eager not to trip on her
high heels, which gripped at the sides of her feet. She was never
usually one for wearing high heels. She didn't dress up all that
often. Right now, in high heels, a black skirt, showing a little
more of her legs than she was comfortable with, and a black top,

she felt pretty well dressed compared to usual. All because of a guy. All because of a damned guy.

She looked down at her phone. Five past twelve. Hell. She was late already. She was *never* late for anything. That's something Adam and her had discussed since they'd started chatting online. They were both punctual people, and they both hated lateness. Great first impression to make. Really put her damned foot in it this time.

She bustled past a crowd of tourists taking photographs of a building. She wasn't far off, but in high heels and with the mass of obstacles ahead of her, she felt so far away.

She'd got chatting to Adam by accident, more than anything. She had a breakup a year ago, and then all the crap happened with the ULTRAs. She lost her sister in one of those battles. Kelly wasn't just a sister, she was a best friend. She'd died by accident, sure, one of the many collateral victims of the ULTRAs' wars. But Annabelle couldn't help feeling angry at the ULTRAs for taking her away, even if they hadn't intended to. Even if it had been an accident.

Then when she was at her lowest, Adam just appeared online. He told her he'd added her by mistake, but they just got chatting from that point on. Adam seemed to understand Annabelle. He really seemed to get her problems and actually showed a desire to meet her, which was also something.

She'd been unsure at first. She was still hurt. She didn't want to rush into anything.

But then she'd jumped in with both feet, and now she wasn't looking back.

All around her, she heard the chatter and laughter of people. The sounds of conversation made her feel uneasy. She'd never been a fan of crowds or anything like that. As much as she loved Miami, her dream was to live up in the San Juans, or somewhere like that, a whole island to herself. She wanted to be a writer, so that perfect solitude would suit her to a tee.

She saw Tommy's Beachside Diner up ahead and her stomach did a somersault. She was almost there. She looked at her watch again. Eight minutes past twelve now. Damn. Late.

But come on. She wasn't totally late. And after all their going on about hating lateness, it'd be something to break the ice with. Annabelle really felt like she needed to break the ice with something. She wasn't the most comfortable conversation starter. She preferred to jump into existing conversations. Hopefully, Adam would have plenty to say.

She got closer to the diner, felt a bit of sweat on her forehead. Shit. She'd been sweating. It'd stain her makeup. It'd run down her face and make her look stupid. She'd smell. She'd—

She felt her high heel give way under her left foot.

She saw herself falling toward the concrete in slow motion. But the embarrassment covered her fast. She wanted to stop time. To pause reality. To bring it all to a halt.

But she fell face-flat onto the ground.

She twisted over. Her left ankle was still and not easy to move. One of her high heels had snapped completely, and her black shirt was ripped at the bottom. She was covered in dust and the remnants of a chili dog someone had dropped.

She ignored the sniggers and struggled to her feet, her cheeks on fire. She bit her lip and did everything she could to avoid crying. She wanted to go home. She wanted to get away from here. She'd embarrassed herself, destroyed her look. What was Adam going to think about her now?

But still, she forced herself to take a few deep breaths. She walked to the front of the diner.

She held her breath and looked through the window.

The diner was empty. Completely empty, except for an old man at the back reading *USA Today*.

He definitely didn't look like Adam.

He wasn't her date.

Annabelle lifted her phone, messaged Adam and asked where he was. He was always so quick to reply. Literally took seconds, all the time.

But this time, the seconds went on. And the seconds stretched to minutes. Before she knew it, it was half twelve, and there was still no sign of Adam.

She felt the tears start to surface at the corners of her eyes. She felt her teeth start to shake, and her fists tensed.

Inside, she felt total rage.

Rage and embarrassment.

And she felt something else, too.

Something building up inside.

She stormed back in the direction she'd come from. That idiot. He'd stood her up. He was just the same as all the others. He was—

A massive explosion ripped through the street behind her.

She fell flat again. She struggled onto her back.

The diner had blown up completely. Alarms went off. People ran away in a frenzied chaos.

A crumpled, burning copy of *USA Today* rested by the door.

Annabelle felt something weird amidst all the chaos. She didn't feel afraid, as the smell of smoke and the taste of burning filled the air. She felt... relieved. It was weird to describe. Like all her anger, embarrassment and upset had exploded, right when that building had exploded...

Her teeth chattering, she started to lift herself to her feet when someone grabbed her arm.

"Annabelle?"

She looked up at the guy holding her arm.

There was no doubt about his curly, black hair. There was

no doubt about his muscular body, and his smile, mature beyond his eighteen years.

And those green eyes.

Those gorgeous green eyes.

"Adam. I—"

"Come on," Adam said, easing Annabelle to her feet. He put a gentle hand on her back. "There's a lot we need to discuss."

He walked Annabelle away from the scene of the explosion as the sirens started to approach, and weirdly, Annabelle didn't feel afraid, or confused.

She just felt powerful.

Adam made her feel powerful.

[2]

N *airobi, Kenya*

ROSE N'GOYE WOULDN'T HAVE VISITED the mall today if she knew how it was going to turn out.

It was warm outside, too warm for her. Her grandchildren wanted to go to the park to play, but she was too old for that now. So she'd brought them here for ice cream instead. She wasn't planning on staying here long. Just into the mall, ice cream, and out. She didn't like the mall too much. She didn't like being surrounded by so many people like this. Especially not after the attacks several years ago.

They were on the second floor. The ice-cream place had moved. Her grandchildren, Amani and Hasina, were running ahead of her. "You two slow down. Don't be causing trouble."

Amani and Hasina ignored her like all young children ignored their grandparents.

She listened to people chattering around her. She could

smell fries cooking at a nearby café. She was amazed how westernized this place was becoming. She knew Kenya was one of the more progressive African nations, but even Kenya had come a long way in her eighty years on this earth.

"It's over here, Grandma!" Amani shouted, pointing at a stall in the distance.

"I want strawberry!" Hasina called.

"I want vanilla!"

"Vanilla's for bores."

"Okay, okay," Rose said, hobbling up beside them. "You won't be getting anything if you don't remember your manners. Now come on, let's get your ice creams and get you back to your mother."

She approached the ice cream stall and started salivating. She saw the ice cream dipped in chocolate and hazelnut, and it reminded her of the first time she'd ever met Atieno. They'd gone for ice cream and sat in the sun by Lake Victoria. Only Atieno had a nut in his ice cream, and he was allergic. So it wasn't the perfect first date.

But to Rose, it was perfect in her memory. She would never forget it. And she would never forget Atieno.

The ice cream man smiled at Hasina and Amani as they ran up to the stall. "What can I get for you two fine young things?"

Rose smiled back as she walked up to the stall. "We'll have—"

She didn't finish what she was saying, because everyone sprinted in her direction, screaming.

They ran into the ice cream cart and knocked it over.

Rose didn't understand the chaos or the pandemonium at first. It didn't seem real to her.

But when she heard the gunshots ripping through the mall, she knew exactly what was happening.

History was repeating itself.

"Kids!" she shouted.

She ran over to Amani and Hasina with what little strength she still had in her withered old body.

"What's happening, Grandma?" Hasina asked.

"It's—We have to get out of here. We have to get a long way from here."

Rose looked over her shoulder and what she saw made her mouth fill with the bitter tang of vomit.

People were being shot at.

Ordinary, good people were falling over.

And men dressed in black were approaching wielding Kalashnikovs.

"Quick!"

She ran away from the men with the fleeing crowd. The sounds of the screams were deafening. All around her, people tumbled down; many got trampled on. She hoped it wouldn't be her or her grandchildren next, but there was no knowing what might happen.

She got to the top of the escalators. The exit door wasn't too far away. Already, people were making their way out of it. It wasn't going to be easy, but she could make this. They could all make this. "Just keep hold of my hand and—"

An explosion ripped through the mall.

It was right at the exit door.

People flew back in the air. The smell of burning filled the mall, as another chorus of screams erupted. Still, the men progressed, firing their Kalashnikovs into more and more of the terrified crowd. And as Rose stood there holding the hands of her children, a part of her wondered if maybe this was the end after all.

No.

No, she was fighting for her grandchildren.

She turned around and pushed against the crowd that was

still eager to get down the escalators. "There's a fire exit!" she shouted, gesturing at more of the massive crowd to go in the direction she was heading. But none of them seemed to be listening to her, all of them so afraid. "At the back! There's a fire exit!"

She battled her way through the crowd of people. Their mass was suffocating, and she felt like a sardine. All the time though, she gripped onto the hands of her grandchildren. She was getting them out of here, getting them to safety. And sure, they would be afraid for the rest of their lives. They would be scarred. But at least they'd be alive.

She reached the back of the crowd and made a break for the fire exit, which she knew was right at the back of the music store.

When she got there, in the middle of this silent store, she opened the door. An alarm sounded. More chaos erupted inside the mall.

"Now come on," Rose said.

Amani was crying. So too was Hasina.

She crouched down and put her hands on their shoulders. "We have to be brave. We're getting out of here and we're getting away."

"I'm scared, Grandma," Hasina said.

Rose kissed Hasina's forehead. "I know you're scared. I'm scared too. But it's when we're scared that we do the best things sometimes, hmm? It's when we're scared of the roller coasters that we go on them, and then we always get to the other side, don't we?"

"I don't like roller coasters," Amani said.

Rose squeezed his shoulder. "Well this one's almost finished. Come on. We have to—"

"Wait right there."

The voice came from the front of the music store.

There was a man standing there. He was dressed all in black.

He was pointing his Kalashnikov at Rose.

He walked slowly in Rose's direction, his boots thudding against the floor.

"My grandchildren," Rose said. "Please. They mean no harm. They are innocent."

"You do not tell me who is and isn't innocent. That is for God to decide."

"Please!" Rose cried. She threw herself in front of the man, landing at his feet. "I beg you. Take my life. But do not take the lives of my grandchildren. They are such beautiful creatures. So harmless. Please."

Rose didn't hear anything from the man for a while.

When she looked up, she saw he was pointing the Kalashnikov right at her forehead.

"I think I'll take you up on that offer," he said.

He squeezed the trigger.

Rose closed her eyes.

She heard a bang.

But after that bang, she didn't feel anything. Her ears rang. Her head felt heavy. But she definitely hadn't felt anything.

She opened her eyes.

She squinted when she saw what was in front of her. It was as if the man had been paused pulling that trigger.

All of the bullets were hovering slowly in midair toward Rose.

All of them had been frozen.

It was then that she noticed a blurriness outside the music store. The sign of fighting. The sounds of the Kalashnikovs were fading.

Then she saw a young man walk around from the back of the man with the Kalashnikov.

His face was covered. He was dressed in a black suit with an eagle emblem on the front.

Rose knew exactly who he was.

"You should really, really not have pulled that trigger," the young man said.

He lifted his hands and rammed the bullets back at the man with the gun.

They flew through him. Pierced holes in him.

They sent him staggering back to the floor.

The young man looked at the fallen man, and then he turned and looked at Rose and her grandchildren.

He held out a hand.

"Come on," Glacies—Kyle Peters—said. "Let's get you out of here."

3

Of all the kinds of attacks in the world, terrorist attacks were definitely my least favorite.

I felt my stomach churn. No wonder. It was nine o clock back in America and I still hadn't had any damned breakfast. I'd been sitting in a diner with Ellicia too, but that'd gone to shit the second I'd gone to bite into my juicy axon and seen the news of the attack in Kenya.

I'd shot back home. Suited up in my new, bulletproof Glacies gear, funded by a coalition of governments around the world.

Then I'd headed to Kenya and... well, here I was.

In the midst of stopping a terrorist attack, sure. But bacon-free.

Dammit.

I walked out of the music store and headed back to the main shopping center. There were lots of bodies on the floor, which made my skin crawl. People were crying. I tried to ignore the blood. I had to focus. I had a job to do.

The good thing? The gunmen all seemed to be down. I'd dealt with them one by one, taken them down rapidly. Sure, the last one had come close to putting some bullets into a poor old woman and her grandkids, but I'd stopped him too and helped them out of the fire escape.

But I wasn't leaving yet because I wasn't finished.

I walked over the fallen bodies and looked down onto the bottom floor of the mall.

I saw the fire burning over by the main door. I'd seen that on the news, and it was at that moment that I knew there was something more to this terrorist attack than just terrorists. The way that explosion had erupted in thin air. And the way a girl had stood outside while that'd happened.

There was no doubt in my mind that an ULTRA was responsible for this.

I heard gunfire and felt bullets pelt my left side.

I spun around. The bullets bounced off my costume, but they still packed a punch. Over by the back of the mall, three more armed men ran out, all of them with Kalashnikovs, all of them firing in my direction.

I walked towards them, activating a shield around myself. "Seriously?"

Then I lifted them into the air, opened up a wormhole underneath them, effortlessly, and cast them into it.

I could still hear their screams echoing long after they'd disappeared.

I heard something else then. Something behind me. Footsteps.

When I turned around, I saw another man with a gun.

Only...

"Oh sh..."

This man didn't just have a Kalashnikov.

He had a rocket launcher.

He fired the rocket at me. I tried to gain my footing and push back against it, but it was already close to me.

I gritted my teeth together. Held it in midair.

Then the guy fired two more rockets.

My grip on that first rocket slipped.

I focused on it again. But focusing on more than one wasn't easy.

Besides, I could hear more footsteps approaching behind. I could still hear wounded people screaming. I was stuck. Totally cornered.

I closed my eyes and took a deep breath.

"You should just give up while you have the chance."

I went invisible.

Then I hovered up into the air, still holding on to those rockets.

The terrorists looked around, bemused and frightened.

I lowered myself down behind the back of the one with the rocket launcher. I grabbed a piece of fallen wire, turned that invisible too, and wrapped it around his ankle as delicately as I could.

Then I wrapped the next end of the wire around the first of the rockets, still hovering in midair.

"Where the hell'd he go?" one of the other gunmen shouted, running toward their friend. They stopped when they saw the rockets. "Shit. Are they—"

"Still explosive?" I said, clicking my fingers and deactivating my invisibility as I hovered above them. "Absolutely."

I let my grip of the rockets loose.

The man went flying along with them, attached by the wire.

The rockets slammed into the other gunmen.

All of them disappeared in the explosion.

I smiled at what I'd done. Then I heard my phone ringing, and I knew I was in trouble.

"Kyle?" Cassie said. "Don't tell me you're where I think you are."

"I couldn't just leave these people to die, sis."

"I know that's not why you're really there. It's because of her, isn't it?"

"So you saw her too?"

"Come back here. We're given our orders by the government now."

"And I'm sure the Kenyan people would appreciate me being here right now."

"You've no idea what you're doing. What kind of shit you're opening up."

I saw her, then. Saw her running along the bottom floor. She disappeared through a door, and I heard her footsteps descending some steps from right up here. The rogue ULTRA. "Hold that thought."

I canceled the call and teleported myself down to that door.

I stepped behind it, being careful not to walk into any kind of traps. When I saw it was all clear, I descended the stairs, the lights flickering above me. I kept on going. There was no sign of the ULTRA. None at all.

I started to worry this was some kind of trap when I saw her standing alone in a room opposite me.

She had dark hair, and she was dressed in a torn black shirt and a black skirt. She had nice legs; I had to admit that. She was wearing high heels.

"Don't think we've met before," I said.

The girl, about eighteen, smiled. "Annabelle. But you can just call me Chaos."

"And what's a girl like you doing attacking the innocent people of this mall?"

Her smile widened some more. "I was hoping I'd get to meet you. I was right."

I felt uneasy about the way Chaos said that. "What's that supposed to mean?"

She looked up at the roof above her. "What is it worth, to you, to stop me from leaving this place and killing more people?"

I tightened my fists. "Everything."

She looked back down at me and the smile dropped from her face. "Good."

She shot up into the roof and vanished.

I looked up. I couldn't let her just get away.

I flew into the roof, right where she'd disappeared to.

I didn't get far.

An explosion blasted through the building.

It ruptured the mall into tiny pieces.

It sent me flying out of the shopping center, too weak to even cushion my fall.

4

I woke to the taste of blood.

Sunlight burned against my closed eyes. I didn't want to open them for fear of what I might see. The back of my head ached, and my body felt broken. I knew I could heal myself, eventually, but right now I didn't feel strong enough to do anything, or fix anything at all.

I could hear muffled sirens somewhere in the distance, and behind my blood-blocked nose, I could smell smoke. In my gut, a sickening guilt, as the memory of how events unfolded replayed around my mind.

I had flown up toward the roof of the mall, following the ULTRA called Chaos.

But right after I'd flown up there, something had happened. There was an explosion. An explosion that threw me right out of the mall and onto the gravel by the side of it.

I didn't want to open my eyes. I didn't want to see what I'd done.

But I had to.

I opened my eyes and immediately my stomach dropped.

In the distance, through the bright light of the beaming sun,

I saw the mall. Or at least, I saw what was left of it. Smoke plumed up into the sky. The flashing lights of emergency services surrounded it, as fire services attempted to hose the flames into oblivion. Around the mall, I could see people standing, some of them on stretchers. They looked devastated. Shell shocked.

But they were alive. That was something.

What was bothering me were the people still in there. The ones who hadn't got away.

I had to go back in there and I had to help them. I couldn't just leave them to die.

I tried to teleport myself back inside the mall but I fell to my knees. Pain covered my body. My back ached. My stomach felt like knives were sticking into it. I looked down and saw I was covered in blood. My arms were broken. That explosion had booted me out of the mall and I'd hit the ground with the slightest of shields, but it wasn't enough to protect me completely.

I took deep breaths in through my nose and out through my mouth, but even that wasn't easy. Sharp pains shot through the right side of my body. I wondered if I'd cracked a rib, pierced a lung. Ugh. Just the thought of it made me feel sick.

There was one thing I absolutely needed to do though. That was go back into that mall and help whoever was still inside there.

And to do that, I needed to be strong. I needed my powers.

Screw the fact that I hadn't been ordered to go on this mission by the government in the first place.

This was *my* mission.

I closed my eyes and focused my attention on the tips of my toes. I felt the pain there, and I started to pour in my anger and my energy. I felt it creeping up my body, fixing me, piece by piece. It wasn't easy. My breathing got more difficult. The pain intensified with every inch of myself I tried to fix. But fixing myself was what I had to do. I couldn't just roll over and give up.

I tasted more blood in my mouth when I reached my ribs. I felt that sharp pain intensifying as I focused even more on fixing myself. I had to fight through it. I had to battle through.

I felt my throat closing up and my muscles tightening as I focused on the rib, which I knew now was snapped.

I squeezed my eyes shut tighter.

Held my breath.

Then I shifted it back into place.

I fell to my knees. The pain of putting the bone back into place had taken it out of me completely. But now I was in pain, I quickly moved on to my arms, then healed the scratches and cuts on my head.

When I'd done, crouching there, gasping, I looked up at the mall.

I knew what I had to do.

I teleported my way back inside the mall.

It hurt. And right away, when I got inside, I was overwhelmed by the sheer amount of flames. The smoke was suffocating and turned me into a coughing mess within seconds. I created a shield around myself so I wouldn't be affected by the smoke, but visibility was still difficult.

I looked around for movement. There had to be some survivors in here. There had to be someone.

But the further I got through the mall, past the abandoned shops, through the food court, I didn't see any movement at all, and the fear in my gut intensified.

I got to the middle of the court and looked up when a bad feeling surrounded me.

I looked at that music store I'd stood in not long ago. I'd helped the woman called Rose and her grandchildren out through the fire escape. The explosion couldn't have been long after that. I just had to hope they'd made it out in time.

I flew up to that top floor, then walked towards the music store. All of the CDs and vinyl had toppled over, covering the floor. There were flames right by the fire door. The explosion must've hit this place too. I had to hope they were okay.

I walked through that door, keeping my shield activated. I looked down the steps, my heart thumping. I couldn't see anyone there. That had to be a good sign, right?

Then just as I turned away, I noticed movement.

I looked further down the steps and focused on where I'd seen the movement.

There were three people. An older woman. A boy. A girl.

I knew right away that they were Rose and her grand-children.

I appeared beside them and put my arms around the children. "Hey. Let's get you..."

The children were crying.

Rose was completely still.

A wave of grief covered me. I'd told Rose to leave via the fire escape. I hadn't got her out of here myself. I'd gone chasing after an ULTRA instead of focusing on saving people. Rose had died because of me.

I choked back the tears and put my arms around all of them. "It's okay. Let's get you out of here."

"Grandma," the boy cried. "Granada, wake up. Please, Grandma, wake up."

I swallowed a lump in my throat. Then I teleported Rose's body and her grandchildren outside. I dropped them in the grass, where it was safe.

I heard booing. Heard shouting.

I wasn't sure what the noises were. Not right away. It just didn't register because it wasn't something I was used to.

But when I looked up at the crowd surrounding the mall, I realized what was happening.

People looking angry. They were pointing at me, cursing at me.

They were angry at me.

I stood in front of the burning mall—the mall I'd come to protect—and I listened to the shouts of the crowd.

I wasn't the hero in their eyes.

I wasn't Glacies, who'd saved the world from Saint.

I was the enemy.

[5]

I f there was one place I really didn't like being, it was in
the White House.
 Because a visit to the White House meant one thing: I
was in deep shit.

The first time I'd been called to the White House soon after
defeating Saint, I'd been in nerdy heaven. I couldn't believe that
I was finally being allowed into this place. Well, not just
allowed, but I was a part of this place. The Resistance had been
hired by the government to protect world peace. The idea was
American, originally, but it had spread way beyond that and
become a global union. I'd visited the United Nations, NATO.
You name it, I'd been there. But there was still something ulti-
mately magical about the White House. Something so
unmatched.

The late afternoon sun shone in through the tall bay
window at the back of the room I was in. It was nice outside,
and I'd much rather be out there enjoying summer than in here.
Not because I wasn't in awe. There were relics of history all
around me—handwritten letters from Lincoln, original paint-

ings of Kennedy. I was surrounded in a place of such history, but also such treachery.

I'd just rather be outside because I knew I was in big trouble.

I might be privately tutored these days, with my Glacies responsibilities deemed more important than college. But that didn't mean the sickening feeling only a detention brought was gone for good.

In fact, it was much scarier than ever when the stakes were higher.

Vice President Holloway walked back and forth opposite me. He was a short man, with graying hair, and a face that could flick from election-winning charm to total anger in the space of a second. The public didn't often see that anger, and I figured that's why he'd won so many elections. There were rumors that he was totally brutal on his staff, but he was a hard worker, so that was another reason he'd been in office so long.

He was also the man in charge of keeping ULTRAs like me in check.

The longer Holloway went without speaking, the more uneasy I grew. I scratched at my arms, cleared my throat. I'd been in trouble with Holloway a couple of times in the past, the second time in a lot more trouble, and he'd spent a lot longer musing. I figured the longer he took to muse, the more shit I was in.

He'd been musing forever.

Finally, he spun around and looked at me with those piercing blue eyes.

"Why?"

His question threw me, and filled my mouth with a bitter taste. "I—I—"

"You broke procedure."

"I did what I thought was right."

"You acted rash."

"I had to act rash. There was a terrorist attack. I had to do something."

"No. You don't *have* to do anything. You do what you are told. What you are ordered."

"People were dying, Vice President."

"People die everywhere every day. One day, you'll die too. Unless, I dunno. You have some kind of weird ULTRA-y elixir of life inside you."

"I can dream."

Holloway didn't smile. He didn't look amused, not even slightly. "You are young. You don't understand politics. Public image is just as important as action itself. In fact, screw that. It's more important."

"Public image isn't as important as saving lives."

"You didn't save lives."

"I stopped a terror attack."

"No," Holloway said, growing visibly more agitated. He was right in my face now. "You caused an explosion."

"It was an acc—"

"Don't even say that word. Just watch this."

He spun around and punched the power button on a remote. A large widescreen television came to life. News was rolling.

The footage was in the streets of Kenya. People were holding effigies of ULTRAs like me. They were beating them, burning them. Then the news flicked to more images of more protests like this. A tearful woman held up a placard. *"Who Polices the Police?"*

"You're the enemy in their eyes. You and all your kind."

I shook my head. "If I hadn't done anything, people would've been furious."

"But they wouldn't see you as actively involved in murder, Kyle."

I shook my head. I didn't want to accept Holloway's words. It was a bitter pill to swallow.

"Look," Holloway said, interlinking his fingers and walking back around the desk. "I won't pretend I don't understand. It must be difficult having all those powers of yours and not being able to act on them."

"You've no idea," I said.

"But I do. I have an idea, because I am the Vice President of the United States. I see war in the Middle East. I see conflict in South America. I want to go in there and sort it out. I want to, but I don't, because I understand there's an order to the world. An order that has to be respected."

"It's that order that's got us into this mess in the first place."

Holloway smirked and shook his head. "You've a lot to learn before you become a politician, Kyle. Don't attempt to do my job for me."

Holloway went quiet again and resumed staring out of his window. Great. More musing.

Eventually, he broke the silence. "It was the wrong thing to do, and the people blame you for it. Dress it up however you want. We've had this conversation before, and we won't have it again. You're on your final warning, Kyle."

I knew what that final warning was. He was threatening to cut me from the Resistance because I was "too disruptive". "And what the hell are you going to do about me? Arrest me? Give me a detention?"

Holloway glared at me. "I can do far worse things than arrest you."

"Like?"

"Like turning you into even more of an enemy than you're turning yourself into already."

I mulled over Holloway's words as he walked towards his office door and opened it.

I resisted the urge to continue arguing and made my way to the door.

He put a hand on my shoulder. "Take some goddamned responsibility and grow the hell up, Kyle. The people of the world depend on it."

I took in a shaky breath, and then I forced a smile. "Goodbye, Vice President."

I walked out of the office, and security escorted me away.

Outside the gates of the White House, I saw my sister, Cassie, standing there waiting for me, arms folded. She didn't look impressed.

"You really screwed up this time, didn't you?"

6

"I was just trying to do the right thing."

"The right thing by who?"

"The people."

"Really? So why weren't you in Tokyo?"

"Tokyo?"

"Yes, Kyle. Tokyo."

"Why would I be in Tokyo?"

"There was an armed robbery. Three people were taken hostage. All of them died."

A bitter taste filled my mouth. "I—"

"And what about Bali?"

"What about Bali?"

"Eight people trekking in the hills. They got cut off from the outside world in extreme weather. Two of them died."

I shook my head. "I didn't see that."

"You didn't see it, or you chose not to see?"

"What's that supposed to mean, Cassie?"

Cassie tutted. She leaned back against her chair. We were in a coffee shop just outside of Vancouver. It was a quiet place, and one we could always rely on to avoid any kind of attention.

Usually, the smell of the coffee was so calming and appealing. But right now I wanted anything but to be able to smell it. I didn't want to be having this conversation. I wanted Cassie to believe in me. "You weren't in Tokyo because there was no suspicion of ULTRA involvement. You weren't in Bali because there was no suspicion of ULTRA involvement."

She glared at me as I tightened my hands around my boiling hot coffee cup. If there was one thing I admired in my sister, it was her reluctance to embrace a pseudonym. Said they were "for kids." "And?"

"Don't pretend you didn't see those stories, Kyle. You were in Kenya because you saw an ULTRA going rogue, and you saw red."

I sighed, and leaned across the table. "I still don't see why that's such a crime."

"In itself, it's not a crime. But we have a job to do. We accepted a job to serve the interests of the world governments."

"And saving people from an ULTRA-led attack in Kenya *wasn't* in the world's interests?"

"We don't make the rules."

"That's no excuse for just standing by and watching."

"No. And you went in there and didn't save anybody."

"I stopped the attack."

"And triggered an explosion in the first place."

"That was a mistake."

"So correct me if I'm wrong, but you didn't only trigger an explosion that killed many people, but you let the ULTRA called Chaos slip. Right?"

I turned away from Cassie and looked out of the window. It was raining in Vancouver, surprise surprise. But the rain soothed my thoughts, which was what I needed right now.

"All over social media, people are making out like you're the enemy. Like we're both the enemy."

"Screw social media."

"Those people are people from your school, Kyle. People from Staten Island. People from all over the world are starting to worry about what might happen if just one of us breaks procedure one more time. They've been through it with Saint twice already. They don't want to go through it again. You can't blame them for worrying."

I leaned back on my chair. Cassie had a point. It was only natural that people were worried about the ULTRAs after what'd happened with Saint. But still, it frustrated me. "They need to get over the past and let it go."

"Could you get over the past and let it go if you'd lost someone to the ULTRAs?"

A knot in my stomach, I said, "We have lost people to the ULTRAs."

"Exactly," Cassie said. "And if I remember rightly, you hunted down Saint to the end of the world to punish him for what happened to... to Mom and to me. So you can understand the skepticism."

"I just think people need a little more trust; that's all."

"You don't just click your fingers and get trust, bro. Trust is earned. You've got to work toward it. That's what we're doing by grouping together with the government. That's what we're building toward. We have to show we're in control of ourselves. We have to show people can believe in us. That we can be responsible. Only then can we ever hope to win the people over completely."

I felt sick about the things Cassie was saying. "The Cassie I knew wouldn't just leave people to die."

"And the Kyle I knew was too chickenshit to fight for anyone. I guess we can say we've all changed."

I stood up and walked away from the table. I wasn't taking this anymore.

Cassie's chair scraped the floor. "Whatever you do, whenever you act, remember that every single action is under public scrutiny."

"I don't care about public scrutiny. I'm doing what I can to help people. Why isn't that enough?"

"Well I do care about public scrutiny," Cassie said. "And when you act, it reflects on all of us. So just think about that before you go on another ULTRA-hunt of yours and kill a load of people in the process."

"What is your problem?" I shouted.

Cassie frowned. "Kyle?"

"I saved you. I brought you back. I put everything into bringing you back and now..." I shook my head and started to walk away.

Cassie put a hand on my arm.

I brushed it away.

"Hey," she said.

I turned around and reluctantly looked into her eyes.

She half-smiled at me. Her eyes were so similar to the sadness that'd been in them the day she'd "died." "I'm thankful for what you did for me. Really. But this isn't about you or me, Kyle. Not anymore. This is about doing what's right for the world. And it might not be easy. Nobody ever said it was going to be easy. But it's what's right. And I worry what'll happen to all of us if you keep on like this."

I opened my mouth to say something back to Cassie. To apologize to her. To tell her I was just a scared kid, really. I'd been thrown into this sea of responsibility and wasn't sure whether I could swim without armbands. I wasn't even sure I *wanted* to swim. "I'm going away for a bit," I said. "See you around."

"Oh, Kyle."

I teleported back to our Staten Island home before Cassie

could follow me. A bit bad, leaving her there, really. She hadn't mastered teleportation as well as me, and she wasn't as fast a flyer. But she'd find her way back eventually.

I walked over to my locked cabinet, cracked the padlock away, and then tore through several layers of security. I looked down at my fresh Glacies outfit. I started to put it on when I heard footsteps behind me.

I spun around.

"Shit," I said. "You should know not to creep up on me like that."

Daniel Septer emerged from the shadows at the far side of my bedroom. "We need to talk," he said. "Right now."

7

I sat beside Daniel in the middle of the Australian outback and hoped to God he had a good reason for bringing me here.

The sunset was a thing of beauty. All around, I saw the red rock of desert, a vast expanse stretching right ahead. It was the kind of place that if I somehow lost my powers, I wouldn't escape. I was way too far removed from reality to get away from here. And in a way, that scared me.

As did the thought of all the spiders, snakes, and lizards waiting to bite.

I heard a crack. When I looked to my right, I saw Daniel Septer—Nycto—had opened a beer can and was sipping it back, some of it dripping down the side of the can.

I glared at him. Eventually, he turned to me and frowned back. "What?"

"Beer?"

Daniel lifted it. "Yeah. Beer. Want some?"

"You're not old enough to drink beer."

Daniel snorted. "Kyle, we're two of the most powerful

ULTRAs on the planet. We can do whatever we damn well please."

"You... you shouldn't be drinking and powering."

"Drinking and powering?"

I nodded, like there was such a thing.

Daniel sniggered a bit and turned his head back to face the setting sun. "That's your problem, bro. You need to let yourself go a little. Loosen those shoulders of yours. Can't be comfortable being that tight."

I looked away and cleared my dry throat. Truth be told, I fancied trying a beer, but I knew I shouldn't. I guess I was still a bit of a bluenose in that way. Suddenly becoming an ULTRA hadn't done much to change that. "Don't tell me you brought me here for a beer and a sit in the sun."

"Well it's nice, ain't it?"

Daniel smiled at me. When I didn't smile back, he shook his head and gulped back more of that beer. "We're alcohol resistant anyway. Jeez."

He tossed the can off the edge of the rock we were sitting on and zapped at it in midair.

He missed, and the can fell to the rocks below.

"Not that alcohol resistant," I said.

Daniel didn't say anything back to that. "There's some weird shit going on, Kyle. Some strange developments."

"'Strange developments'? I thought you decided not to join the official Resistance?"

"And I'm proud of that decision when I see you and the rest of 'em all tied up by the laws of the world. Seriously, that can't feel good."

"It keeps us in check," I lied, trying not to blush.

"Don't bullshit me, Kyle. You can't bullshit me. I know damn well you won't like the way things are."

I shrugged. "It's the way things have to be."

"For you, maybe. But anyway. I've been coming across a lot of ULTRAs."

"A lot of ULTRAs?"

"Ones I've never seen before."

"Well, not everyone joined the official Resistance."

"No, but these ones are different. I've seen at least five of them crop up that I honestly didn't know existed."

"Why is that so weird?"

"Why? Because it means there's more than we first thought."

"That's not so weird. We only unlocked our powers when we were a little older."

"But we're Orion's sons," Daniel said. "Maybe we were different."

My throat tightened when Daniel said "Orion". It was still a sore spot between us, and forever would be. Orion, the greatest ULTRA to have ever lived—the *first* Hero—was our father. He'd stood by our side as we tried to take down Saint upon his resurgence. Only we'd lost him.

Daniel had stood by and watched as Saint hurtled him through a wormhole.

I'd never forgive him for it. I'd never forget.

"There's others, too. Others who've only unlocked their powers when they were older."

"Alright. Give me my moment, at least."

I nodded. "So say there is something weird going on," I said. "What d'you think it is?"

Daniel shrugged. "I dunno. I was hoping you'd know that."

"You were hoping *I'd* know?"

"Well you are working for the Resistance. Don't you get like, super-government-technology? Or are you all so tied up that they don't even let you play with their toys, either?"

I stood up and started to walk away.

"Kyle, wait. I'm sorry. I'm sorry."

"There's no reason for me to be here," I said. Although I wasn't exactly keen on rushing back to reality, not now the world hated me even more for the events at the Kenyan mall.

"You need to look into this ULTRA situation. Something isn't right."

"I'll handle it."

"You'll handle it? 'Cause you're not doing a very good job of handling anything else right now."

I turned around and tensed my fists. I felt a combination of nerves and anger spiraling inside me. "What?"

Daniel didn't look intimidated by me. He was one of the few who didn't. "You messed up at the mall. And it isn't the first time you've messed up. No wonder people are turning on you and the Resistance. Starting to feel pretty good about not getting myself involved."

I wanted to turn away before I said anything I regretted; before I did anything rash.

But I couldn't help myself.

I lifted my hands and punched the new can of beer from Daniel's hands.

He glanced around at me. Then he caught the beer in midair with his telekinesis. "Not a good idea."

"You owe your life to me. I saved you. I didn't just spare you, but I saved you. Don't ever forget that."

"You did save my life. I accept that." He pulled back his beer and took another sip, and then he walked toward me. "But something's coming. Something very big. And I just hope you and your little team of soldiers are ready for the storm when it finally arrives."

"You should..."

I didn't finish my words.

Daniel disappeared.

The beer fell to the ground where he'd stood, perfectly upright.

I looked down at that beer can. Then I looked up at the orange sun as it made its final descent, simmering against the vast landscape.

As I stared into it, preparing to head back home as the heat diminished, I couldn't let that final thought go.

I hope you're ready for the storm when it finally arrives...

[8]

Chaos kept her head down. She didn't want to draw any unnecessary attention. Or any attention, for that matter.

The Evoque nightclub in Tokyo was loud and busy enough for her to blend into the crowd. All around her, neon strobe lights pulsated, people dancing and partying on the floor. She could barely hear herself think, which again, was good news, because it meant that everyone else's senses would be distorted even more than her. She could hone her hearing on a particular person if they were speaking to her. She'd been doing it for fun the whole night, jumping from conversation to conversation. Even if they were at the opposite side of the club, she could focus.

She thought back to the events earlier that week. The mall in Kenya. She felt bad about what'd happened. Truth be told, she wasn't expecting the gunmen to be in there. That wasn't part of the plan she'd agreed.

And the explosion. Yes, she could cause explosions. That was one of the gifts she'd discovered that day at the diner four months ago and had been training to hone ever since.

But that explosion at the mall wasn't her.

In the first days of meeting Adam, their relationship had been... well, pretty blissful. He saw something in her. He told her he'd not *given* her abilities, but rather he'd *unlocked* them.

She liked that. Especially after all the hell she'd been through with family recently. It made her feel special.

She knew now that the whole unlocking powers thing was bullshit. As much as she still felt *something* for Adam, she knew she wasn't his special snowflake anymore. And as much as she liked his plan for changing the world and shifting the power from the Resistance to the people—especially after what happened to her sister in the midst of an ULTRA conflict—she just wasn't sure it was the reality she'd wanted anymore.

Especially not after what happened at the mall.

She'd thought about changing her allegiance. But she knew it was already too late. The world was talking about her. She was involved in the attack on the Kenyan mall. And sure, the plan to set Glacies up had gone pretty well, framed him as even more of a bad guy in the eyes of the masses. But it just wasn't what she'd agreed, the whole killing thing.

So she was here to meet *him*.

She was here to quit.

She looked around, the strobes giving her a headache. She saw guys leaning against the bar with open-necked shirts. At the opposite side of the bar, a couple of Westerners looking over at her with interest. She tutted, then looked past those. She wasn't legally able to drink, at seventeen. Adam had friends running this place, though, so she was always allowed in. She'd get in even if she were turned away, though. That was another one of her little tricks, too. She didn't exactly need ID to get into anywhere. She could just walk through the wall.

Which is exactly what she'd done when she'd disappeared from the Kenyan mall.

That brought a bitter taste to her mouth too; now she saw those events for what they were. Her part of the agreement was that she'd destroy a door, cause a bit of furor and then go onto the lower floor of the mall, then lure Glacies into chasing her. And she'd done that. She'd done everything she was asked.

She thought it was particularly weird when she was asked to make it then look like she'd flown upwards when really she'd flown downwards. But she trusted Adam. He'd been trustworthy as long as she'd known him. She couldn't exactly dispute it.

But when she saw the explosion, when she saw the, for want of a better word, chaos, she knew right then that she was messing around in something way, way out of her comfort zone.

She was an ULTRA now, sure. But the Resistance wasn't for her. Too many shackles. Too much order. Too undemocratic.

Plus, her mentor—the guy she looked up to so much—hated everything the Resistance stood for.

She looked down at her watch. Quarter past twelve. He was fifteen minutes late. That wasn't like him. He had a way of getting under her skin in a way that nobody ever had. Chaos wondered if she was the only one. He had a way with words. A charming manner. A confidence beyond his years.

And he had grand ideas.

She was about to get up and leave when she saw him standing right at the back of the nightclub.

She felt her skin crawl. He was wearing a black suit, all black, with a black shirt and tie underneath. He had dark hair tied back into a man-bun, which he pulled off way better than anyone Chaos had ever known. He was muscular, and although he had a bit of a baby face and was only eighteen, he carried himself like a man who had been around for a long time.

Adam smiled, and Chaos felt herself melt a little inside.

She got up from the bar and walked toward him. When she

did, he turned around and left. She felt the frustration of the chase building again as she budged past the people in the night-club. She could swear some of them were looking at her closely like they knew exactly who she was.

She reached the back of the nightclub and stepped out of the fire door.

He was standing outside in the uncharacteristically silent street. He was looking up at the night sky.

Chaos walked toward him.

"You wanted to see me?"

He turned around, and she felt his charming allure all over again.

Chaos couldn't look him in the eye. If she looked him in the eye, she wouldn't be able to tell him exactly what she had to tell him. She nodded, staring at the ground. "I—"

"Before you start, I just want you to know how proud I am of you," he said, putting a hand on her shoulder. "You did so well at the mall."

"People died."

Adam shook his head. "Sometimes people have to die for others to be saved."

"You really believe that?"

He smiled, and that smile filled him with total warmth. "Yes, I do."

Chaos had never thought that way. In fact, she'd only been going by the name of Chaos since Adam asked her to. Before that, she was Annabelle.

"Well, I don't. I think it was wrong."

Adam pulled his hand away and frowned. "You agreed to do what you did."

"I agreed to something completely different. I didn't agree to kill people. Just to block one of the doors then confuse Glacies. I did that. But you... you sent gunmen in there. You rigged the place with explosives."

Adam lifted his hands. "I didn't do a thing, Chaos. I'm not in control of the militants in that area. Both of us know it's a dangerous location."

"So you're saying it was just a coincidence that there was a load of gunmen there? You're saying it was just chance that Glacies happened to fly into a bomb? Because that explosion wasn't me. You know that, Adam."

"I'm saying that sometimes in life, we have to let chance take its course. And chance really is taking its course right now. It's on the brink of rising up for good. Don't forget what I gave you, Annabelle."

Chaos looked down at the ground. The booming bass from the nightclub thumped on behind her. She remembered the explosion at the cafe when she was going to date Adam. Her anger had caused that. She hadn't been an ULTRA before that day. But when she came across Adam, something had happened. "I don't forget. I won't ever forget."

"Then you'll carry on as we planned. Soon you'll see the world's better for it."

Chaos wanted to agree. She wanted to stay by Adam's side.

Instead, she shook her head, looking right into his eyes. "No."

He frowned. "What?"

"I said no. Just... just no. I can't do this. It isn't me."

"But you're so—"

"It's over, Adam."

Chaos turned around and walked down the alleyway. She wanted to get out of the darkness and onto the main street. She didn't want to be with Adam anymore.

"We can't just let you go," he said.

Chaos looked back.

Adam wasn't alone anymore.

Behind him, there were people.

The more Chaos looked at them, the more they creeped her out. Some of these people she recognized from inside the night-club. Only they weren't enjoying themselves anymore. They weren't just in there having a drink and a laugh.

Their hands were sparking with blue energy.

Chaos turned around and started to run.

More people were in front of her now.

Blocking her way out of the alleyway.

"You don't just walk away with a gift like the one you have," Adam said.

Chaos felt a sharp pain stab her back.

She fell to the ground, hit the sidewalk hard.

She rolled over, tried to fight back with her powers. But she couldn't move. Her powers were weak. She felt all out of energy, all out of life.

And all around her, the crowd stood.

In the middle of them, a smiling Adam.

"I'm on the way to becoming a messiah, darling," he said. "And a messiah doesn't take rejection lightly."

"Ple—"

The crowd lifted their hands.

They fired their energy at Chaos, collectively.

She felt the energy fading from her body.

The last thing she saw was a little rat poking its head up from the gutter beside her.

Then nothing.

9

"**D**ude, since when have you been such a daredevil?"

I smiled when I heard Damon's voice. I'd taken him and Avi with me to an inactive volcano in Iceland. We were in our caving gear and surrounded by total darkness.

Well. We would be if it weren't for the light beaming from my forehead.

And not a flashlight either.

"Man, wait. Seriously. Do not run away from me. Do not abandon me."

"I wish I'd stayed at home," Avi said, fear in his voice. "Take us home."

I turned around and looked back at Damon and Avi.

"You're gonna have to step inside the cave at some point," I said.

They both stood at the mouth of the cave, barely a foot over the threshold. I couldn't help but smile at them standing there so fearful. Even though none of us had ever exactly been daredevils, I always used to be the most cautious of all of us. So seeing them cowering right now, yeah. It was a pleasant surprise.

"Could we not just, like, do normal things like go to the cinema or something?" Damon asked.

"I hear there's a new milkshake place," Avi said. "We could go back and check that out."

I turned around and looked at the darkened cave ahead. "All my powers, all the places I can take you, and you want to be at home slurping milkshake?"

"More than you could ever imagine, man."

I shook my head and sighed. I walked back over to Damon and Avi. Their breath frosted in the cold, and specks of snow covered their helmets. I put my hands on both of their shoulders. "Okay," I said. "I think I know the place."

"You do?"

"Oh, yeah. A great place. You'll love it. Especially if you're a fan of thrills."

"Space?"

I frowned. "What?"

"Space," Damon said. "Like, Jupiter or something."

"You don't want to stick around an Icelandic cave, but you want to visit Jupiter?"

I saw Damon's eyes glazing over, like the cogs in his head were spinning. "Well, maybe not. Have you ever been, though?"

"Been where?"

"To Jupiter."

I wanted to tell Damon that of course I'd not been to Jupiter. I didn't have a death wish. But I had to admit it wasn't a bad idea. I'd have to at least try heading into space at some stage. "We're not going to Jupiter," I said. "But somewhere else hot. Somewhere to get the pulse racing."

"Wait—"

Before Damon could finish, I teleported us over to the other side of Iceland.

"Jesus!"

We were hovering right above the mouth of an *active* volcano. Hekla. I'd quickly created an invisible barrier between us so we couldn't fall, but Damon and Avi were already both running to the sides.

I created a couple more invisible barriers around the perimeter. "You don't want to run," I said.

"Of course I want to goddamned run," Damon said. "Get me out of—"

He hit the invisible barrier and tumbled back onto the invisible floor beneath him.

I'd never heard him scream so loud, which triggered Avi to scream even louder.

Tears of laughter streamed down my cheeks.

I walked over to them and put a hopefully comforting hand on their backs. "Now this is what we're gonna do."

"Just get us home, Kyle," Avi spluttered.

"We're going to go ten feet down into this volcano."

"No!"

"We're going to go ten feet, and if you still want to go home then, I'll take you home."

Damon shook his head. Avi shook his. Both of them looked like they were going to puke.

"Five feet," I said.

"Minus five feet, bro," Avi said.

"Come on. Five feet's not even your own height. You can do that, can't you?"

"I don't know, man," Damon said.

"You can do it. And when you do it, you'll feel amazing. Trust me. You'll feel like you can take on the world."

"Is this how you get your kicks? Dipping your toes into volcanoes?"

"Five feet," I said. "You ready?"

Damon and Avi sighed and shook their heads. They looked totally defeated.

"Okay," I said, easing them to the middle of the volcano. "You like roller coasters, right?"

"What—"

I banished the invisible floor from beneath us.

We fell right down. I heard Avi and Damon both squealing. I felt something warm hit my face, and I knew it had to be sick.

As we fell, the wind blowing against me, the heat of the volcano getting hotter, I felt totally at ease with what I was doing. A total thrill. I was having a laugh with my friends. That was the main thing that mattered in the world. It was a shame Ellicia was ill today. For their sakes, more than anything. I might've taken it easier on them if she wasn't.

When we'd fallen quite a way, and I'd heard enough of my friends' screams, I stuck my hands out to create a bouncy invisible barrier right beneath us.

Nothing happened.

I tried again. Threw everything I had into forming some kind of barrier.

Again, nothing happened.

I felt my stomach turn. Below, I could see the orange glow of lava getting closer, as the smoke intensified. I looked to my side and saw Damon and Avi both hurtling past me, heading towards the lava first.

Shit.

I fired again. Tried to fire again and again, but nothing was happening.

I watched my friends inch closer to that lava, and I realized right then that I'd done something wrong. Very wrong.

And then they hit a spongy blanket of thin air, myself following not long after, and we all went flying right back up towards the mouth of the volcano.

I eased our landing as we fell back out of the volcano's mouth. Avi and Damon were on their knees coughing, puking. I brushed some of the dust from my hair and rested my hands on my legs. I couldn't help laughing. "How was that?" I said. "How frigging awesome was—"

"That was *not* cool," Damon said.

He stood right in front of me. He didn't look impressed at all. He was crying, and Avi didn't look too far off tears either.

"Hey," I said, lifting my hands. "It was just a bit of fun."

"For you, maybe. But we could've died."

"You wouldn't have died."

"You were playing games with our lives, man," Avi said. "That's *not* on."

"Oh, seriously," I said. "Get a grip. I could save your lives with the click of a finger. I *did* save your lives with the click of a finger."

"Just like you saved those lives in Kenya, hmm?" Damon said.

I looked into Damon's eyes. I was surprised to hear him mention Kenya. It was the first time he'd ever pulled me up for anything like this before. "What's that got to do with anything?"

I thought Damon might hold back at that point, but he clearly wasn't happy. "You play games with people's lives all the time. It's just what you do now, isn't it?"

"You have no idea what happened in Kenya."

"I know people died!" he shouted. "And I know everyone's saying it was you who let the entire Resistance down. So that's enough."

I was literally speechless.

Damon dusted himself down. "Take us away from here."

"Damon—"

"You know, I didn't want to tell you this because you're my best friend. But Ellicia isn't ill. She isn't ill at all. She just didn't want to come here because she's afraid of you. Of what you're turning into."

That halted my words more than anything else. I felt myself choking up. Ellicia was afraid of me? Why would she be afraid of me? What did she have to fear?

"I'm doing my best," I said. "You have to understand that. It's not easy. I'm doing what I can."

"I miss the old Kyle, bro," Avi said.

"You miss the old me? That wimp who got bullied all the time? Who let people get the better of him?"

"No," Avi said. "I miss the Kyle who really cared about other people. I miss that Kyle. Now get us home. Please."

I stood there for a few seconds, the wind intensifying around me. The smell of sulfur was strong from the volcano. My best friends were turning against me. Even my girlfriend was afraid of me. What was my life coming to?

I sighed and walked towards Damon and Avi. "You two have nothing to worry about. I swear."

I teleported us back down to the side of the volcano.

I was about to teleport the three of us away from here for good when I saw we weren't alone.

There were people all around us with crowbars and hammers. Some of them looked big and tough, the kind of people I really didn't want to have to mess with.

We were surrounded.

10

I looked at the mass of people surrounding me and I was positive they weren't here to just talk.

Some of them were holding crowbars. Other, broken off metal pipes. It was weird seeing so many people down here by the side of an Icelandic volcano. It freaked me out in many ways. How had they found me? How had they got here? I'd made my best efforts to get here under the radar, as I always did. So how had they caught on to me?

"Kyle?"

I looked to my right and saw Damon by my side. Avi was by his. They were both shaking. They'd pretend it was because of the cold, no doubt, but I knew they were afraid.

I looked back at the surrounding crowd and lifted my hands. "There's no need for any trouble here."

The crowd just peered back at me, eyes narrowed. There was something strange about them. Something distinctly... other. They looked like normal people. Men with bushy beards, well built.

But the look in their eyes was so cold.

And the weapons in their hands weren't much more reassuring.

"Is that right?"

I scanned across the crowd to see who'd spoken. It took me a second for my eyes to land on a thick-chested man with wispy blond hair. He was holding an ax. "Yes," I said, trying to cover the concern I had for this situation. "Now if you'll excuse us—"

"I wouldn't try to get away if I was you."

I narrowed my eyes. I could feel the agitation building inside me. "What did you just say?"

A smirk twitched at the sides of the man's face. "You heard."

I felt my fists tense. I couldn't believe how this man was speaking to me, and how everyone was just standing by him and letting him. He was too confident. Too cocky. Too sure of himself.

I wasn't used to people standing up to me like this.

"After all," the man continued, "you're 'Glacies'. And Glacies isn't gonna do a thing to hurt another human now, is he?"

The rest of the crowd chuckled. The main guy's accent was strange. It was American, but with a Scandinavian twinge.

"Don't try me," I said.

"Oh," the man said, his eyes widening and a grin stretching across his face. "Is that the great Glacies making a *threat?*"

"You haven't even heard the start of it," I said.

Damon tugged my arm. "Kyle, let's just go—"

"See if you got that head of yours out of your ass for five damned minutes, you'd realize that there's something coming. Something you should be very, very afraid of. You probably don't know what it is yet. You're probably close to figuring it out. But when it arrives, I promise you, you'll feel it, and you'll know."

My skin went cold. When this guy spoke those words, I

couldn't help thinking of Daniel, and what he'd said to me as we'd sat in the middle of the Australian outback.

"Something's coming. Something very big. And I just hope you and your little team of soldiers are ready for the storm when it finally arrives."

I wanted to fight back against this crowd. I knew I could obliterate—or at least neutralize them—in an instant.

But then I remembered all the damage I'd caused already, all the negativity that surrounded me in the public eye, and I didn't want to make that any worse than it already was.

I cleared my throat and smiled. "Been a pleasure speaking with you, gents. But now me and my friends are getting the hell outta—"

I felt something smack against my back, felt electricity cripple my skin, tighten around my throat.

I fell to my knees and hit my head on the rocks beneath me. I tried to fire back at these people, but the electricity crippling me was too strong. They'd shot me with some kind of anti-energy device like the ones Saint used to use to restrain ULTRAs in his tower. I was stronger than those devices. I could battle through them.

But just as I started to compose myself, taking a few deep breaths, I felt a boot smack against my ribs.

Then another one kicked my face.

Then a metal pole hit my head.

I took more and more punches and hits, shielding myself with the slightest powers I could. I could taste blood though, and my nose was blocked, so the shield couldn't be working completely.

I spun onto my back and tried to drag myself out from this animalistic crowd. When I looked up at them, saw the anger in their eyes, I realized they saw me as a monster. This was what they thought was right. This was what they thought I deserved.

"Kyle!"

I heard Avi's scream and it made my skin crawl.

He was being beaten up too. So was Damon.

I tensed my jaws, ground my teeth together, the punches against my shield getting heavier.

I pressed down against my teeth so hard that a molar slipped out of place.

"Kyle, please!"

I focused on Avi and Damon's pain—pain I couldn't allow to continue.

Then I let out a cry.

I felt the power blast out of my body, from between my lips. It flew up to the people above me. It was a strength I'd never felt before, and the second it left my body, I was sure that I'd taken a step too far.

The people around me stopped swinging their weapons, kicking out at me.

Their eyes rolled into the backs of their skulls.

Their muscles went weak.

They dropped to the ground.

Every one of them.

I stayed on my back for a few seconds, the wind whirring around me. In the distance, I could hear chatter, and I realized a crowd of shocked looking tourists was staring up at me and the scene around me in total amazement.

I got up, ignoring them, and walked over to Damon and Avi. They had to be okay. I couldn't face it if they weren't. I'd never live with myself.

I stopped walking when I saw them.

They were both lying there on their sides.

Blood dripped down from Avi's nose.

Damon was covered in bruises.

They both looked up at me in fear.

"Guys—"

"Go," Damon said.

I frowned. Then I heard the crowd behind me stirring. When I looked, I saw them jeering and booing at me like I was the enemy all over again.

I looked at the ground, at the fallen people—still fallen—and I knew exactly why.

"We've got to get—"

"Just go," Damon said. His voice was shaky. He sounded weak. But above anything, he sounded certain. Totally, terrifyingly certain.

I swallowed a lump in my throat as the tourists kept their focus on me.

I looked at my friends, beaten and wounded all because of me.

And I looked at the mass of bodies all around me.

This was who I was.

This was what I was.

This was Kyle Peters.

This was Glacies.

11

Adam looked at the crowd of frantic people and he smiled.

The dust had barely settled at the foot of Hekla after the brutal attack on Kyle Peters and his friends. Specks of snow fell heavier from the sky now, covering up the blood on the ground. All around, Adam saw media reporting at the scene—media from all over the world, with the same topic on their lips: what Kyle Peters, their "savior", had done to the poor souls who'd attacked him.

Of course, Adam knew the truth, as he walked away from the foot of the volcano. He'd set those people on Kyle. He'd promised them great riches—the greatest of riches, and riches that he'd proven to them that he could provide, if they just did this *one* thing for him.

Unfortunately for them, Kyle had retaliated.

But they'd died a part of the greater good.

They'd died for a very, very important reason.

He took a deep breath of the icy air and walked further away from the scene of the crime. Iceland was nice. It reminded him of a trip he took to Europe with his parents around a year ago. They went on a family vacation, with plans to go to Scotland, then down through England, over to France. But Iceland always stuck with Adam.

He remembered the majesty of it. Remembered the beauty. Even though his visit was only a year ago, it seemed so long ago, with everything that'd happened since. The main thing that stood out to him was the relationship with his father. He'd never really bonded with Dad in the same way as Mom. But on that vacation, they'd done everything together. They'd gone on a road trip along the south shore, to black sand beaches and quaint, undiscovered villages. They'd gone swimming in the Blue Lagoon. They'd even gone snorkeling between the tectonic plates. Everything seemed good. Everything seemed fine between Dad and him, for the first time in a long time.

Then Kyle Peters and his idiot brother had flown into the plane they were boarding from Reykjavik to Edinburgh just before it took off, and neither of his parents had made it.

He wondered where Kyle Peters was now, whether he was afraid. Soon, he would be in hiding. Everything he cared about and loved was falling away, just like everything Adam loved fell away too, and very soon he'd have nothing left at all.

That was all part of Adam's plan.

He thought about the bloodied, terrified looks on the faces of Kyle's friends, and how they'd reluctantly disappeared with him, back to whatever world they'd come from. But Adam was good at reading people, and he knew for a fact they would never stand by Kyle in the same way again. Not after what they'd been through. Not after what he'd put them through.

Then he looked at the glove on his arm.

He'd been fortunate getting hold of it. Very fortunate. The good thing about Saint's rule was that it made many no-go areas suddenly free-for-alls.

Adam had done his research. He'd made plans.

Then he'd stolen what he needed.

He knew he'd have to be patient. He knew it might be years before his plan came to fruition.

Fortunately for him, it was becoming reality way, way sooner than he could ever have dreamed.

He looked back at the foot of the mountain. Saw the flashing lights of an ambulance wheeling the bodies inside. He saw the police trying to keep people away from the scene. He heard the words "Glacies" and "ULTRAs" so many times it made his head hurt.

But that was good.

It meant his plan was coming together.

He chuckled a little, unable to contain his excitement for the next stage of the plan. For his great awakening. An awakening that would not only shock Kyle, but would upset the entire world order.

And Adam would be respected for it.

He would be adored for it.

He held his breath and took a final breath of the cool Icelandic air.

Then he disappeared across the globe, back to America, back to his army.

He looked at the people all standing opposite him. His followers. There were hundreds of them now, and soon there'd be hundreds more. They were growing, slowly at first. But gradually, the army was getting larger. Adam was mastering his gift.

Many of them had anti-energy guns, too.

Guns that he'd purchased for a pittance of their worth using a stash of Bitcoins on the deep web. Guns that the general public didn't like to accept were out there.

Enough of them to take down the Resistance and get to Kyle Peters, Glacies.

He looked at his hundreds of followers.

Soon, hundreds would become thousands.

And thousands would...

Well. He'd see how it worked out.

He smiled at his people, all of them with their beautiful powers. With that naivety that was even more powerful than understanding.

He smiled at them, one by one.

"It's almost time," he said.

[12]

I was back in the White House.

Last time, I knew I was in trouble.

This time, well. I knew I was in big, big trouble.

The sky had grayed outside, which captured both my mood and the rest of the Resistance who had been called in with me. I'd learned a term in one of my final English classes. "Pathetic fallacy." It was a term to describe what happened when the weather reflected the general mood. Of course it was rubbish—writers and directors used it to evoke a certain mood to the reader and viewers, and it was more for dramatic impact and all that hoo-ha than anything else.

But right now, it felt like there was serious truth in "pathetic fallacy."

I didn't know what was coming, but I knew it couldn't be good.

Vice President Holloway stood opposite me, just like he had when I'd last been in here not long ago at all. He stared out of his window, totally silent. The silence had dragged on a long, long time. I mean, last time was a lengthy wait, but this time was on another level. I knew that couldn't be good news. If I didn't already know that. Which obviously I did.

Eventually, Holloway turned around and looked right at me. He wasn't red and angry. He was pale. Totally pale.

"Speak," he said.

I looked around at Cassie, Ember, Roadrunner, and a few of the other Resistance members by my side. We were all in here, every single one of us. Which worried me even more. They weren't exactly going to be my biggest fans after this.

When I looked back at Holloway, I saw again that he was looking right at me.

"I didn't intend to—"

"No bullcrap. What did you do?"

I felt the back of my neck heating up. "What happened out there. We were set upon. It wasn't supposed to—"

"Seriously. Cut the crap, right this second. Tell me straight what happened. You surely aren't too dumb to realize just how much crap you are in right now, and just how much crap you've dragged the rest of your team into."

I heard a few grumbles of discontent behind me.

I lowered my head and took a deep breath of the clammy air as the rain rattled heavily against Holloway's windows. "I was out there with friends."

"What were you doing with friends?"

I shrugged. "Erm, doing what normal teenagers do?"

"You aren't a normal teenager. That's your first mistake."

I shook my head. I knew I wasn't a normal teenager. I didn't need reminding. "We were leaving when we were surrounded."

"So you attacked them?"

"No! No of course I didn't. I tried to get away. But then one of them fired one of those anti-energy things at me. Before I knew it, I was on the ground being beaten. I didn't have a lot of strength in me. Just enough to hold them off for a while."

"So you were shielding yourself," Holloway said, as if he was weighing up my every word. "And then suddenly you're on the attack?"

"I heard my friends being beaten up. I... I didn't mean to hurt anyone."

"Well you did. You hurt a lot of people. Even killed some."

I shook my head, my throat tightening. All around me, I saw the disapproving, judging glances of my colleagues. "I had to help my friends. I couldn't just watch them die."

"You should know better than to react in the way that you did. Especially with all the negative attention we've been getting lately."

"That's all this is about?" I said, my skin tingling with heat. "Negative attention?"

"You have responsibilities," Holloway said.

"Damn right I have responsibilities. I have responsibilities to my best damned friends to keep them alive."

"The interesting thing here, Mr. Peters, is that the problems are always with *you*. The rest of your colleagues, sure, they have the odd incident here and there. But you just keep on making the same mistakes. You're acting recklessly. And in the eyes of the people, you're doing more harm than good. All of you."

I saw Holloway look around at more of the Resistance then. He hadn't said what I knew he wanted to say, not yet. But I knew what he was implying. "You're punishing us all for my mistakes?"

Holloway sighed. "I've been your biggest champion all along. All of you. The last thing I want to do is concede defeat where the Resistance is concerned. Because honestly, I still believe you're a force for great good."

"But?"

"But right now I think it'd make a lot of sense if you stepped out of the limelight for a while. All of you."

I didn't know what to say. Part of me could understand what Holloway was saying. But another part—a bigger part—couldn't help hearing Daniel's words echoing in my mind.

"When I see you and the rest of 'em all tied up by the laws of the world... Seriously, that can't feel good."

He was right. I was tied down by these people.

"You use us when it suits, but when it doesn't quite fit in with your agenda, you don't want us anywhere nearby."

"Let's keep this polite so we can move as smoothly as possible, please."

"You don't want to make enemies of us, Holloway. You don't want to make enemies of any of us."

Holloway's eyes narrowed then. "What?"

"I said you don't want to make enemies of us."

A smile stretched across Holloway's face. "You can't force people to like you, 'Glacies'. You can't force people or ULTRAs to follow you. That's what Saint did, and look how that worked out."

"Don't compare me to Saint. Just don't."

"You need to take responsibility for your actions in order to be liked. In order to be respected. And that starts right now."

I felt a massive invisible force slam against me. My ears rang, and I dropped to my knees. Behind me, I saw other members of the Resistance on their knees too. Ember. Roadrunner. Stone. All of them writhing around, their powers suppressed. All of them struggling.

Holloway walked up to me and lifted my chin. His face was covered with regret. "I don't want to do this. But for now, I think it's best that we take all of you into a facility for a while."

"Don't."

"It's for your own good. Your own benefit."

"Please..."

I looked to my right and I saw Cassie lying flat on her stomach. She was wincing, struggling. I'd done this. I'd caused this mess.

Holloway put a hand on my back.

"I'm sorry, Mr. Peters. I really am."

He walked over to his window as he called on his guards to come in and take us away.

I looked up at him. Tried to fight back against him, as he stood there, his outline against the window.

I threw everything I had into—

Then I heard it.

A humming noise outside the window. A shout.

Holloway frowned. He turned around to the glass. "What—"

He didn't finish what he was saying.

A massive explosion tore apart the wall of his office, smashed his window.

Vice President Holloway disintegrated before our eyes.

In his place, a guy stood.

He couldn't have been much older than me. He was well-built, though, and dressed in a sharp looking suit. He looked at me with his piercing green eyes and smiled.

Behind him, I saw a group of people.

Then, on the ground below, I saw more people gathering around to watch.

The media gathering around to watch.

"Hello, Glacies," the guy said. "Nice to finally meet face to face. I'm Adam."

I realized then that whatever had been suppressing our powers had dropped.

Someone beside me—Rhino—realized too. "Let us out of—"

One of the people beside Adam lifted their hands and shot him from existence.

I tightened my fists then. Everyone behind me joined as the smell of smoke grew.

The people behind Adam all activated their powers, too. A classic Western stand-off. I noticed some of them were holding government issue anti-energy guns. Weapons that were put in place to neutralize the ULTRAs temporarily. Take enough hits from those guns, and we'd be paralyzed for a while.

I didn't know where Adam had got them from exactly, but I could wager a bet that he'd stolen them from the government. Or bought them underground.

Adam chuckled as he studied the stand-off. "Now now. There's no need for any more violence. Not today. Today is a day of peace, not of violence."

He turned around to face the ULTRAs behind him, and the crowd of people around the White House.

"Today is the day we get our world back."

"Who the hell do you think you are?" Roadrunner asked.

Adam turned back around. He smiled that charming smile, revealing his perfect white teeth. "Who am I?" he said. "Let's just see who I am, shall we?"

He put his hands on the sides of Roadrunner's head and she let out a scream.

I tried to throw myself at her, but a flurry of those anti-energy bullets slammed into me and into everyone else who tried to run to Roadrunner's aid.

Roadrunner perched on her knees. A blue energy lifted from her skin. She was totally pale. She couldn't stop screaming.

"People are the ones who should have the decision to control their own futures," Adam said, intensifying his grip on Roadrunner's head. "People are the ones who should elect their gods, not the government. And people are the ones with the power, now. People have their world back. And with my help, the people's powers are going to get even stronger."

He pulled his hands away from Roadrunner's head and she fell to her knees, eyes closed.

He walked away from her. I tried to go after him, or to Roadrunner, but my powers were still crippled.

He walked over to the opening where the window had once been. He looked down at the mass of people below, staring up at him. He took in the view, then lifted his hands.

Then he fired at a small group to his right.

I felt my defensiveness kicking in again. He was firing at people for no reason. He was...

Then I realized the people he'd fired at were still standing.

Not only that, but they were running.

Running fast.

Just like Roadrunner used to.

The crowd started to chatter loudly amongst themselves. A nervous excitement had control of them, as Adam turned around and looked me in the eye, smile across his face.

"The powers are returning to the people. Just where they should've been all along. Now. Who's next?"

The group behind him, joined by more people from the crowd outside, activated their powers.

Powers that Adam had taken away from ULTRAs.

Powers that he'd given to people.

People who hated the Resistance.

13

I struggled against the anti-energy resistance suffocating my powers as the crowd of newly-powered humans marched toward me.

I couldn't take my eyes off them. Watching them walk toward me was one of the scariest things I'd ever witnessed. These were supposed to be the people who respected me. These were the people I'd worked so hard to protect ever since I'd discovered my ULTRA abilities.

And now they were coming for me and getting ready to capture me so Adam could take my powers away.

I listened to the sounds of panic behind me. All of the Resistance were on their knees now, their skin sparkling with the anti-energy crackling across it. They were all down, they were all wounded. They had no chance of fighting free of that neutralizing energy. I was the only one who was powerful enough to, and even I couldn't make it right now.

They were still looking at me with terrified eyes like I was the answer. Like somehow, I had the solution.

But the harsh reality was, I was just as trapped as the rest of them.

I was just as screwed as the rest of them.

I looked back to the front of the Resistance and saw Road-runner curled up in the fetal position.

She was alive. She'd shifted since Adam took her powers away and redistributed them to a watching crowd. But she was clearly in pain, both physically and mentally. She looked like she wanted the ground to open up beneath her and take her far, far away from here. And I couldn't help feeling total guilt for the position she was in; for what my recklessness had done to so many ULTRAs I cared so much about.

"We can't just give up."

I heard Stone's voice, but I didn't know where exactly it came from. He sounded frightened. Uncharacteristically frightened. That scared me even more.

"Kyle. Don't you dare give up. You brought this on. You fix it."

I rolled over and saw Adam's cronies a few feet away from me. I heard what Stone was saying, but how the hell was I supposed to fight free?

Then I saw Adam right in the middle of the crowd, holding hands with joyous looking people. They were falling to their knees before him like he was some kind of messiah.

I knew right then that he was the key. Even if I didn't deal with all these newly converted ULTRAs, if I took down Adam, then at least it'd be like a Band-Aid on a wound. I could think about tidying up this mess. The Resistance could still stand, and it could fight back against those who were going wayward with their powers.

It wouldn't be easy. But it was our duty to protect the world, whether the world wanted it or not.

I forced myself to my feet. My head throbbed with pain. I tried to shift myself across the room to the middle of that crowd, but still, the anti-energy gripped me tighter as more of those bullets hit me.

I took a deep breath and tensed my fists.

I thought of everything that made me angry.

Seeing Adam take Roadrunner's powers away.

Seeing my sister, Cassie, on the floor, struggling to break free.

Seeing myself taking my anger out on all those humans that had been attacking me, Damon and Avi.

I couldn't just give up. I couldn't just—

More anti-energy bullets hit me.

I started to fall down to my knees but managed to rebalance myself. I took some more steadying breaths, then lifted my head and focused on Adam, trying to drag myself towards him to take him down, no matter how ugly it'd be.

I was Kyle Peters.

I was Glacies.

I could defeat him.

I could—

More anti-energy bullets hit me, and this time, I really did collapse.

I rolled onto my back, the shouts and cries of my fellow ULTRAs filling the room as Adam took more of their abilities away and redistributed them.

And then I heard the screams stop, and I saw Adam standing right above me.

He peered down at me with that face that would annoyingly be the gossip of every girl, and he smiled. "How does it feel?"

I was too weak to respond.

He reached down and moved his hand towards my chest. I could feel an energy radiating from it. Like a magnet pulling something out from the center of my body, towards him.

"This is what happens when our politicians and our 'heroes' elect themselves," Adam said. "I'm sorry I have to do this. But I'll make sure I make good use of your powers."

I tried to hold my powers back.

I tried to keep everything from bubbling over the surface.

Then I felt tightness right in the middle of my chest, and as I knew my powers were being snatched away from my body, I screamed.

14

I screamed out as my powers were wrenched from my body.

I squeezed my eyes shut. I couldn't see a thing other than flashing lights behind my eyelids. I could taste the metallic tang of blood. All around me, I heard my scream echoing and the shouts of others as they were rounded up by Adam's newly-powered cronies. My nose was blocked, presumably with blood, so I couldn't breathe very well. My entire body writhed in pain as I felt the power emerging from every inch of it, burning in its intensity.

In a horrifying flash of realization, I saw exactly what was going to happen here. Adam was going to take my powers away.

I couldn't let him do that.

I bit down hard on my bottom lip and tried to clutch back at the powers rising from my body. It took everything—concentration, resistance, agony. And the more I pushed to try and stop my powers being taken away, the more slippery they became.

This was it.

I was becoming Kyle Peters again.

I was going to be a normal kid again.

For a split second, I reveled in that fantasy. After all, a normal life was what I really wanted, wasn't it? Ever since I'd been "gifted" my abilities, I'd moaned on and on about how much I wanted to just live my life as a teenager again, like everyone else.

It should've been a happy moment. But I knew there was nothing positive to come from this.

I needed my powers. The world needed me.

Whether they realized it or not, I was here for their benefit.

I forced my eyes open, as painful as it was.

I saw a fiery, simmering glow rising above me. It was still clinging to my body, like glue, falling away in places. I knew that it was my abilities.

Adam had his hands above me. He was lifting those powers closer. I saw right then the look in his eyes that told me everything I needed to know. He might've been masquerading as a man of the people—a messiah—but he was just another power-hungry asshole like the rest of them.

He was looking at my abilities, and he was pretty much salivating.

I had no doubt he planned to keep my abilities to himself.

I looked back. The Resistance were all surrounded now. Roadrunner was still on her knees looking totally broken. Acid, whose powers you can probably figure out in no time, was flat out on his back. So many other members of the Resistance were down, and looking weak.

I tried to fight back against Adam, but the grip he had on my powers was intense and tight. The more I pushed, the stronger Adam seemed to get.

But Roadrunner.

The Resistance.

Cassie.

It might take it out of me if I fought back. Hell, it might render my powers completely useless.

But I wasn't giving up.

I had to fight.

Otherwise, the Resistance would fall.

I held my breath and looked back up at Adam. "You're not taking them away that easily."

I put every ounce of focus onto all of my love, and all of my anger.

Then I let out a cry.

I wasn't sure it was working at first. I didn't know if I was getting anywhere.

Not until I saw the light slam back into my body, felt it wind me right in the stomach.

Not until Adam tumbled back.

I stood up, then. The anti-energy grip on me had loosened.

I looked back at the Resistance. I saw the rocks spreading across Stone's skin, and the flames on Ember's hands.

I knew right then that they were free of their anti-energy powers.

But only for now.

I teleported over to them and stood with them. I put my arm around Cassie.

"You okay?" she asked.

"I'm okay. It's just—"

"We need to fight these idiots," Stone said, his voice booming. He was fully covered in rocks now.

Opposite, I saw the anti-energy charging from the guns of Adam's people.

Behind them, I saw Adam getting back to his feet.

"We can't," I said.

Stone turned and glared at me. "What?"

I looked down at Roadrunner as she kneeled there. I looked

at the rest of the Resistance, too. So many of them were down. So many of them were wounded.

And those anti-energy weapons were so, so close to being back to charge.

"We can't fight," I said.

"Of course we can goddamned fight."

"If we fight, we risk losing. And if we lose, we lose our powers. We lose... we lose who we are. What we are."

I heard Adam chuckle. He was standing right by the open wall at the opposite side of Mr. Parsons' old office. Outside, on the grounds, which had totally been overthrown, masses of people stayed and watched. "See, you are weak, really. When your powers are at risk, you are weak. Because what are you without your powers, really? You are just normal people. You aren't special snowflakes. Which is why it's time for someone else to police the world. Someone that the people really believe in."

I was about to argue when I heard the chants from outside. They made my skin crawl.

"*Adam!*"

"*Adam!*"

"*Adam!*"

I looked around at the Resistance. I wanted to fight. I wanted to take down Adam and restore order.

But then I looked at Roadrunner, at the stupor she was in, the grief she was in, and I didn't want to become that.

"Well, tough," Stone said, cracking his fists. "If you want my powers, you're gonna have to pull 'em from me yourself."

Adam's smile twitched. "Maybe I will."

He nodded at the people in front of him.

They pulled their anti-energy triggers.

I felt time slow down then. Or rather, I unconsciously slowed it down myself.

I ran to Stone.

Then I grabbed Cassie, then Ember, then Vortex.

I grabbed a few other Resistance members too, got them all as close together as possible as the anti-energy bullets hurtled towards us.

I turned around and started to run for Roadrunner when I realized the bullets were too close.

If I went for Roadrunner, the anti-energy bullets would hit the Resistance, and everything would be over.

If I didn't...

I swallowed a lump in my throat. I felt a tear building in my eye.

"Sorry," I muttered. "Sorry."

Then I stepped up to the group of Resistance I'd managed to bundle together, and I teleported us outside the building, my powers still too weak right now to fully teleport any further.

There was only one thing we could do right now.

Run.

15

W hen I teleported as many of the Resistance as I possibly could away from the White House, we didn't get as far as I'd have liked.

I landed on my right side, my face smacking against the concrete. I winced and rolled over. My head stung, and that taste of blood that'd filled my mouth just moments ago was stronger than before now.

I looked around. We were just around the back of the White House. Shit. I'd tried to teleport us to the other side of the world and this is as far as we'd got.

"What the hell do you think you're doing?"

I turned around and saw Stone opposite me. His voice was booming. Beside him, Cassie, Ember, Vortex, and some of the other Resistance members I was less familiar with. They didn't look impressed. Mostly, they looked confused.

"We can't fight them," I said.

"Bullshit we can't fight them," Stone said. "They attacked us. They—they did something to Roadrunner. We have to go back for her."

I looked up at the building. It'd gone surprisingly quiet inside, which made me wonder if anyone knew we were actually out here. On the street at the other side of the building, I could still hear the crowd chanting Adam's name. "I want to go back. But—"

"But what?" Stone barked. He walked toward me. "You're too chickenshit to go back in there?"

"You have to look at what's happening, Stone," I shouted, my impatience getting the better of me. "Adam can take powers away. He took Roadrunner's powers away. He almost took mine away. If he takes all our powers away, then there is no Resistance left."

"So what do you propose we do, genius? Sit around and wait for him to catch us? Leave Roadrunner in there to..."

He didn't finish what he was saying. I knew what he was implying, though.

"Look," I said, taking a few deep breaths to compose myself —and hopefully compose the others. "We need a plan. A proper plan. But we can't fight back if we don't have our powers. It's as simple as that."

Stone shook his head, but he didn't seem to have an argument this time.

"Kyle's right."

Vortex stepped forward.

"I don't want to agree with him, but I believe he's right."

"I agree," Ember said.

I wasn't expecting that. Ember usually sided with Stone on these things. So to have his support made me feel a lot more positive that we were making the right move.

"Walking away isn't the right answer. But we aren't walking away for good. Just for now. And then we'll be back. We'll take him down. Together."

I nodded, then looked at Cassie.

She stared into my eyes. I got the feeling she wanted to say something. Hell, I got the strangest feeling she wanted to *disagree*. That was the thing with Cassie. She had the same powers as Daniel and me. She just didn't believe in herself as much. All those years in suspended animation had eaten away at her, made her rusty. I believed in her. But she just didn't believe in herself.

And sometimes, that stopped her believing in me.

"Cassie?"

She opened her mouth.

Then a massive explosion rocked this side of the White House.

We flew back. I felt my footing falling but bounced off the ground and into the air, regaining my composure.

"What the hell was that?" Stone said.

We hovered together opposite the source of the explosion.

I didn't have to answer Stone for him to see what'd caused it.

Adam's followers were hovering outside the building. Some of them were holding those anti-energy guns.

And they were getting ready to fire.

I wanted to shoot us away but I saw there was no time to dodge them. I'd have to take some of them down, make it easier for us to escape.

I jolted forward through the air and landed beneath the guy furthest to the left. I swung him around by his ankle, throwing him into his friend.

Three of them fired at me.

I pushed back against the bullets and threw them through the gaping hole in the wall. I saw more of Adam's followers emerging, and some of those anti-energy bullets hit them.

Before I knew it, there was an anti-energy firework display.

And I knew it was only a matter of time before I was caught in the crosshairs.

"We have to drop back!" I called.

I fought off a few more of Adam's followers, but it wasn't easy. I saw more of them emerge, and that's what scared me. The faces. I recognized them from the street below. Some of them had electricity crawling up their hands. Others were jolting through the air, just like Roadrunner had.

They weren't just the first wave of Adam's cronies.

They were the people from the street.

People with powers.

And now they were using those powers to fight against us.

I dodged the punch of a woman, and then I felt her foot connect with my face. I didn't want to fight back, so I dropped further back, alongside the Resistance. With my refreshed powers, I created an invisible shield between them and us. But it wouldn't be enough. It wouldn't hold them off forever.

"What do we do?" Ember asked.

I felt a bitter taste fill my mouth as more and more newly converted people appeared from the hole in the building.

I felt my skin crawl when Adam appeared, Roadrunner's limp body in his arms, a wry smile across his face.

"Roadrunner!" Stone shouted.

He started to bounce forward when I grabbed his arm.

"We do the only thing we can do right now," I said, as the anti-energy bullets and the attack of Adam's followers burned through the shield.

Stone looked at me. He shook his head. "No. You don't take us away. You don't give the hell in. Not now. Not when he's got—"

"It's the only thing we've got," I said.

I closed my eyes.

Held my breath.

Then I focused all my energy on teleporting the whole lot of us away through a wormhole.

This time, we would appear on the other side of the world.

This time, we really were running away.

Only Roadrunner wasn't running with us.

16

Adam watched his army of newly converted humans disappear into the sky in pursuit of Kyle Peters and the rest of his unelected Resistance.

The clouds parted and the sun peeked through. He took a deep breath of the warm summer air and felt a smile stretch across his cheeks. He was on top of the government building which he'd detonated and destroyed just minutes before. The streets were lined with joyous people, celebrating that they finally had someone fighting for their best interests; someone who was all about redistributing powers rather than keeping them bottled away to himself.

He heard a cough. When he looked to his right, he saw Roadrunner lying flat on the roof of the remaining section of the White House beside him.

It was pitiful, seeing an ULTRA who had been so strong now so bereft of powers. Really, she was nothing more than a weak girl now. But that's what she'd always been, too. Just a weak kid who'd suddenly found her strength when she discovered her powers. The world deserved stronger than her. The people deserved it.

"How does it feel?" Adam asked.

He walked up to her and stood over her. He didn't say anything to her, just looking down at her as she lay in front of him.

"To have everything you care about taken away from you. How does that feel?"

"You won't win," Roadrunner gasped.

Adam tilted his head to one side. "Oh, really?"

He stretched out his arm and turned Roadrunner's head to face him. He looked right into her eyes, and he saw tears. But not just tears of upset or disappointment. Not just tears of fear.

Adam saw tears of anger, too.

"Kyle's strong," Roadrunner said. "The Resistance, they're all strong. They'll come back. They'll find a way to defeat you. And they'll get me away from here, too."

Adam sighed. He chuckled a little.

"What's so funny?" Roadrunner gasped.

"Nothing, nothing. Just find it amusing that you're so confident you're even going to be here to save."

He saw the shift in Roadrunner's face then. He saw her look of defiance change to a look of confusion. He saw the subtle dilation of her pupils. "What—"

Adam nodded at the follower beside him.

They tightened their fists.

Roadrunner's eyes rolled back into her skull.

She fell face flat onto the roof, and she went still.

Adam sighed. Then he turned around and looked back up into the clouds at his disappearing armies, the chants of the people surrounding him.

He was going to stop Kyle Peters.

He was going to let the will of the people speak.

And, most important of all, he was going to take control of this world.

He wasn't going to let anyone or anything get in his way.
It started now.

17

This time, my teleportation worked.

We landed in the middle of the Amazon rainforest. I was immediately hit by the humidity of the place, even though I'd visited here before. The tall trees were all around me, thick and suffocating. They were either good places to hide or terrifying prisons. I still wasn't sure exactly.

The sounds of the rainforest were even more terrifying. I could hear the constant chattering of birds and reptiles that I didn't recognize as familiar by any stretch. Sure, I had powers, and I could deal with whatever creepy crawlies came my way. But I was still a normal guy underneath the Glacies guise. I still didn't want any damned spiders crawling on me.

I rested my sweaty hands on my shaky knees and re-gathered my composure. My throat was dry, and the thick, humid air wasn't exactly easy to inhale. I stood there and I closed my heavy eyes. I didn't want to think of anything right now. I didn't want to dwell on any of what had happened. Sure, I knew we needed a plan. But right now I just wanted to lay low more than anything. Regroup.

"So what's the next step?"

Ember's voice dragged me from my moment of solitude. I looked at him, then I saw Stone, Vortex, and Cassie beside him. Behind them, a few more members of the Resistance, Thunder, who could influence the weather, and Detonate, who could create little bombs in her hands and throw them at her enemies. There were a few others, too, but all of them blended together right now.

All of them were looking at me for answers.

"Well, we obviously need to fight back against Adam."

"And how do we do that?" Stone asked.

I swallowed a lump in my dry throat. "That's what we're here for. We're here to figure it out."

"There's no time to figure anything out," Thunder said. He was black, and wore a sparkling white Adidas shirt with dark skinny jeans. If that was his "look," then it was hardly the most superhero I'd ever seen. "Adam's got Roadrunner. We need to—"

"There's not a lot we can do for Roadrunner," I said.

I wasn't sure where those words came from. I didn't like them, either. Because I knew they were true.

"What?" Ember asked.

"Roadrunner," I said, continuing. "She's had her powers taken away. There's not a lot we can do for her."

"We can at least *try* and help her," Vortex said.

I heard the discontent surrounding me, and I felt everything falling apart at the seams. "Look, I realize what the situation is here. I know what we have to do."

"Then tell us," Detonate said. "Tell us what your plan is."

"I..."

"You don't have one, do you?" Ember said.

I sighed and looked to the ground. "We've fought Saint. We defeated him. The most powerful ULTRA in existence and we stopped him. We can defeat this joker."

"But how?" Vortex asked. "How are we supposed to defeat him if we can't even get near to him?"

It was a fair point. And as much as the discontent amongst the ULTRAs upset me, I knew the concerns were perfectly legit. "We'll figure that out."

"What, now?" Ember asked. "We'll figure it out right now, will we?"

"I'm doing my best here."

Stone snorted. "If this is your best, I'd hate to see your worst."

I saw then that every single ULTRA here was looking at me with disappointment. Like I'd been the one to bring this on. "You blame me. Don't you?"

Stone shrugged. "All I'm saying is, if you hadn't gone all batshit reckless, then maybe people would respect you a little more."

"Cassie? What do you think about all this?"

My sister wasn't looking at me. Just at the rainforest floor.

"Cassie?"

She looked up. "I think perhaps it's time we... we took a different route."

"A different route?"

"You deserve a break. A chance for... for fresh leadership."

Cassie's words hurt me more than any of the others. I felt like a javelin had pierced through my chest. *Fresh leadership.* In a polite way, she was telling me exactly what the rest of the Resistance were telling me—that this was my fault, and it was time for someone else to take the reins.

"I just try to do the right thing," I said. "I just... I just wanted what's best for everyone all the time."

"And that's respectful," Vortex said. "But I think perhaps your sister is right. You are the enemy in the eyes of the people.

As long as you're leading us, we're all the enemies. But if we can start again, maybe..."

Vortex might've continued talking, but I didn't hear her.

I just heard the rustling in the trees right behind the Resistance.

I put a finger to my lips and walked towards the source of the rustling.

"What is it?" Cassie asked.

"Didn't you hear that?"

"What?"

I narrowed my eyes and looked all around. I didn't want to use my powers and draw attention to us. "I thought I heard something. I thought I..."

When I turned back around, there was a man looking right at us.

He was dressed in a green T-shirt and wore a camo cap on his head. Beads of sweat covered his narrow face. He narrowed his eyes at me, then looked at the people around me. He didn't look happy that we were on his land.

I raised my hands. "I apologize."

He narrowed his eyes even more—like he didn't understand.

"For coming on your land," I continued. "We're just looking for safety. For shelter. But we'll leave now. We'll leave."

"You don't have to leave."

The voice surprised me. The man spoke fluent English.

I narrowed my eyes. "What do..."

He pulled out a gun and fired at me.

Before I could resist it, I felt paralyzing electricity cover my body.

I fell to my knees.

I couldn't fight back.

I woke up.

I had no idea where I was. My vision was blurred. I wondered if I was back home lying in bed. It wouldn't be the first time I'd had a nightmare like this. I often had nightmares about the darkness. Sometimes, I'd see something in that darkness. The cities of the world burning. People screaming. Running away from... from *something*. I didn't think much of it at the time, but those visions seemed so real. I felt the warmth of the flames against me, and the screams made my skin crawl. I could smell the charred flesh, which brought the taste of vomit to my mouth.

Then I woke up and I'd be in my bedroom and within a few minutes, the dream would be forgotten.

This time though, the darkness didn't disappear as I opened my eyes. I tried to shift my hands, but I was trapped. I felt like my wrists and ankles were tied to something. My head throbbed like I'd got some kind of hangover from using my powers too much. I remembered what Orion once told me about using them. *They age you.* I hadn't shown many signs of that yet, luckily. But with the amount of times I'd used those powers in the

REVENGE OF THE ULTRAS / 87

last year, it wouldn't surprise me if I started showing those signs of aging sometime soon.

I felt a sharp pain in the middle of my chest when I tried to use my powers, radiating from my ankles and my wrists, and I realized I must be tied down with anti-energy bands, which must've been bought off the black market or something. Shit. I could handle them if I put all I had into it, but I wasn't sure how much *all I had* was right now, or whether it was enough.

And then I remembered the rest of the Resistance.

My memory of what'd happened was blurry. I knew someone had walked out of the woods. But then he'd whipped out an anti-energy gun before I had the chance to acknowledge what was happening, and then he'd fired at me.

I'd fallen to the rainforest floor. But I had no idea what'd happened to the rest of the Resistance.

To my sister.

I struggled harder against the ties around my wrists and ankles, but they were just too tight and too repressive. I felt the dread build inside my stomach. There was no knowing what might be happening to my sister and my Resistance family right now, only that it couldn't be good.

I thought of Roadrunner, and I felt guilt all over again.

She'd fallen down.

She'd had her powers taken away from her.

And then we hadn't even gone back to help her because we were too worried about losing our own abilities.

I hoped that wherever she was, she would be okay.

I prayed that at some point, when we got a plan together, we'd be able to help her.

But right now I was trapped, and there wasn't a lot I could do about it.

I held my breath and tried to teleport myself out of these ties.

But then the electricity frazzled my skin, and I felt even weaker.

I gritted my teeth. I couldn't give up on the people I cared about. They might've given up on me, but if anything, that only drove me even more to prove to them they were wrong about me.

I could lead.

I could have control.

I could—

"Yeah. Yeah we've got Glacies. You want him? Yeah, well there's something we want too. No. No, no deal. This is how it is. This is how it's gonna be."

I closed my eyes and held my breath as the footsteps walked around in front of me. It didn't take a genius to figure out this guy was trying to bribe Adam somehow.

"I get it. I know. But that's how we're gonna play things. You give us abilities, we'll give you Glacies. You still there? Yeah. Yeah, I'm here. I'm... Look, you better think carefully how you play this. We won't keep him alive forever."

I heard a bleep of the guy putting a phone down.

Then I heard him walk right up to me.

I kept as still as I possibly could as the guy walked up to me. He pulled the blindfold that was over my head away, so behind my eyelids, there was light. I wanted too much to open my eyes and get a good look at it. But I knew I couldn't risk this guy finding out I was awake. If he did, he'd give me another big dose of that anti-energy, enough to knock me out. He thought the current level was enough. I had to let him believe that.

He leaned right up to my face. I felt the warmth of his skin, smelled the sourness of his breath. "What the hell are we gonna do with you, huh?" he said. "What the hell are we gonna—"

I blasted my powers inwards.

The anti-energy bands exploded, sending a spark crashing against the guy and knocking him onto the grass.

I leaned over him, my breathing weak and my body shaky from turning that energy inward. But I didn't have time to mope. I leaned over the guy and pressed my hands to his neck. "Where the hell are they?"

He didn't say anything. And truth be told, I wasn't sure it mattered. I'd find my friends and family if it were the last thing I did.

I tightened my grip as the man struggled to breathe some more. "Tell me. Where the hell are they?"

He struggled more, then he smiled. "The end's coming. Traitor."

I looked up at the trees. I knew the rest of the Resistance had to be nearby. "I'm sorry for this. Truly."

"What—"

I blasted a small ball of energy into the man's chest.

A wormhole sucked him up and spat him to somewhere else on the planet.

I didn't know where.

In all honesty, I didn't particularly care.

I looked up at the trees and held onto the man's phone.

Then I walked towards the woods.

I was getting the Resistance back.

I wasn't giving up on them.

19

A dam stood on the corner of the dimly lit Staten Island street and looked through the window very closely.

He'd heard rumors that she lived here. She'd moved house after the showdown with Saint, of course, for her own protection more than anything. And outside the apartment block, there were well-built bodyguards. But they'd be no problem for Adam. Not with an army behind him.

He heard horns honking all around him. He had his hood pulled up to cover his face. He didn't want to reveal his identity here, not yet. He was a national—*international*—overnight sensation. As much as he enjoyed the attention, this wasn't a time for drawing attention to himself.

This was a time for planning the next step.

He rubbed his tongue against his furry teeth and tasted a little blood on his gum. He'd got it from Kyle when he'd fought back against him. The little shit had actually resisted the magnetic force of his ability to take powers away.

Bless him. It was just a temporary victory for him.

If word from the rainforest were true, they'd soon have him back in their possession anyway.

He thought about the call he'd got from that group in the Amazon. They'd told him they had Kyle and the rest of the Resistance, and that they would only hand them over if Adam promised to give them advanced powers of their own. Of course Adam had agreed. But that didn't mean he was going to stand by his word. He had a group of his newly converted followers on their way over to the Amazon right now.

And diplomacy wasn't exactly top of the agenda.

Adam was drifting from the whole purpose of his visit when he saw movement behind the window.

She was just as he remembered from the footage at the battle with Saint. Slim. Wore cute glasses that perched right on the edge of her nose. She looked quirky. Exactly Adam's kind of girl.

And maybe she would be his girl when he finally got Kyle Peters out of the way.

Because Kyle Peters was nothing more than a distraction for her. Kyle Peters was not as strong as he liked to think.

Kyle Peters was a lie.

And Adam was going to exploit that lie for all it was worth.

He saw Ellicia Williams look at him as he stood there on the sidewalk, and he looked right back into her eyes from underneath his hood. He saw her chocolate brown hair. Those thick-rimmed glasses sitting on top of her nose. Her beaming blue eyes.

She held eye contact for a few seconds, and Adam worried that maybe he'd freaked her out. Maybe her guard would be up.

Then she looked across the street elsewhere.

She didn't look concerned.

She had no idea.

She disappeared back inside the apartment.

Adam took a deep breath of the humid air.

Then, he walked towards Ellicia's home.

20

It didn't take me long to find the compound where the Resistance were being held prisoner.

The scorching Amazonian sun burned down on the top of my head. Around me, classic Amazon rainforest things, like... well, trees. A hell of a lot of trees. I could hear birds singing and feel the humidity as I breathed in the sweet air. Sweat dripped down the back of my neck. No matter how much I tried to cool myself down with my icy abilities, it was still pretty damned warm.

The compound stuck out like the proverbial sore thumb in the middle of the Amazon rainforest. It was an ugly metal structure, with wire fences and barbed wire around the top of it. I could hear dogs barking in the distance. Beside the compound, I could see people picking something from the plants that I assumed had to be some kind of illegal substance.

Standing at the door were many armed guards.

They weren't just armed with the usual machetes and guns. They had those anti-energy weapons, too. I figured it made sense that gangs had got hold of those weapons, which had the abilities to neutralize ULTRAs. It gave them a sense of power.

They were cropping up all over the world, sold on the darkest corners of the internet. Once a weapon like that got into the hands of the public, they weren't too easy to get off the streets.

I had to watch my step. I had to be very careful. I couldn't put my friends at risk.

I activated my invisibility and edged closer to the compound fences. I watched my step at all times, desperate not to trigger some kind of system that'd alert the guards to my presence. I knew it would be only so long before they went looking for their missing colleague in the woods. And when they didn't find him, I dreaded to think what they might do.

I hovered off the ground and drifted over the fence. There were serious numbers guarding this compound, sure. But they were nothing I hadn't handled before. Nothing I couldn't deal with.

I dropped to the other side of the fence, staying elevated just inches above the ground, and with my invisibility still activated, I hovered closer toward the building.

The closer it got, the more nervous I got. I knew these people weren't ULTRA hunters, and it seemed like they weren't totally with Adam either. They were just doing their job, and their job was to hand over my friends and me in exchange for powers of their own.

I knew how dangerous the greed for power could be. We had to be vigilant.

I was about to hover through the wall inside the compound when I heard the dogs beside me growling.

I looked around at them. They were massive, American pit bull style dogs. Studded chains were draped around their muscly necks. Thick saliva drooled down from their mouths.

They were looking right at me.

I checked to see I was still invisible. I was, so I knew they must be able to smell me somehow.

"What's up, boys?" a man asked in Spanish. Yeah, I'd used my abilities to help me learn other languages. Didn't all heroes? How meta.

I saw him, with a rifle in his arms, walk up to his dogs. One of them barked. One of them thrust against the leash.

I was about to quickly head inside when I heard gunfire in the distance.

The man turned around. "Shit." He went running away from the dogs, in the direction of the gunfire.

A distraction. That was just what I needed right now. It was perfect.

I took the opportunity to avoid teleporting through the wall for fear of what might be on the other side and instead drifted down towards the main entrance. I held my breath, reduced my form so not a single atom would be detectable by any systems they had in place—hopefully—and I moved through the door.

The inside of the complex was vast and mostly empty. It was even hotter in here, the glass ceiling creating a greenhouse effect. It smelled of sweat, badly.

I didn't have to look so far to find out why.

In front of me, masses of people worked away at picking leaves and mashing them up. Further at the back of the compound, I saw a machine working away, as more people chopped leaves into small pieces. The air reeked with a sour, unfamiliar smell. I had no doubts now, from some of the documentaries I'd seen on Netflix, that this was some kind of cocaine operation.

I looked around. The Resistance had to be somewhere in this place. I couldn't see them on show, though, so it made me wonder.

I searched all around but couldn't find them.

And then I saw the door at the back of the compound.

I looked over my shoulder. Outside, the gunfire was getting louder. Definitely some kind of battle going on.

I held my breath and started to open the door.

"Stop."

My muscles tightened. My stomach turned.

I slowly looked over my shoulder.

A woman was standing opposite me.

She was holding a knife.

I started to open my lips to protest when I saw another woman appear beside her.

"I can't stop."

"You have to stop," the woman said, putting a hand on the other woman's back. "For your children. For your family."

I took a deep breath and closed my heavy eyes. I was invisible. They couldn't see me. I had to stay focused.

I moved through the door and made my way down some steps. The further down I got, the cooler it got.

I ended up moving through another door.

Then I saw them.

The Resistance—what was left of it—were in a cell.

Standing opposite them, five men.

All of them had those anti-energy guns raised.

"You ever gonna let us out of here?" Stone grumbled. He was bruised. He looked like he'd taken a beating.

One of the guards grinned, revealing a golden tooth. "Oh you will. You'll be outta here soon. Only we'll have your powers, big man. See how many people you're punching then."

"Not so fast," I said.

I appeared behind the men.

Right away, I activated a wormhole and started to drag them into it.

One of the men fired an anti-energy pulse at me. I saw it

getting closer. It was just inches from singeing my skin and rendering me useless for a short while.

I focused on it, as the men disappeared into the wormhole.

Then I froze it in midair, inches from my face.

It turned to ice. Then it melted and dripped to the floor.

I looked up at the men as they got further through the wormhole.

"You were saying?" I said.

"Please don't—!"

I blasted the men through a wormhole.

Wherever they were going, at least they'd be out of my way for a while.

Careful what you wish for.

I deactivated my invisibility and walked over to the cell. "Come on. We have to get outta here."

"You took your time," Vortex said.

I tried to open the cell door, then stepped back and aimed my powers at it. "Yeah. I was unconscious too."

"Wow," Ember said. "The golden boy's not so perfect after all."

"Let me deal with that," Stone said.

I was about to fire the cell door away when Stone grabbed it with his rocky hands and ripped it away without even breaking a sweat.

"There. Now what?"

I thought about disappearing.

Then I thought about those people working away in awful conditions upstairs. I thought about the woman crying, just desperate to make a tiny bit of cash for her kids. "There's something we need to do first."

I started to make my way up the stairs, the Resistance following closely behind.

I walked out of the door into the main room.

What was waiting for me wasn't exactly what I'd expected.

The guards were all down.

In their place, Adam's followers, no doubt about it.

There were fifty of them.

And they were surrounding us.

21

A dam walked up the stairs towards Ellicia's apartment. It was totally silent in this apartment block. He figured it was a bit of a downgrade from the family home Ellicia used to live in. But at the end of the day, safety was paramount, and Ellicia felt safer away from her home.

Quite cute that she stayed in Staten Island though. As if nobody would find her, eventually.

Adam looked over his shoulder at the doorway. The guards that had stood there lay still, their necks twisted and their eyes bulging. He felt a twinge of sympathy inside. He hadn't enjoyed doing what he did to them. Of course, he hadn't done it first-hand. He didn't have the strength to do things like that, not yet. But one of his followers had done it for him.

But even so, he still felt like he'd been the one to snap their necks. It sparked a strange sense of guilt inside, even though he knew he was fighting the good fight.

He never enjoyed taking anyone down. It just didn't fit in with the ethical code he'd had instilled in him from a very young age. His mom had always told him when he was annoyed or mad at someone, to get inside their heads and imagine why they might be acting the way they were. When she'd first told him that, Adam found the idea pretty cool. Getting inside someone's head was like a superpower, and Adam had always wanted superpowers.

But the older he'd got, the more truth he saw in his mom's words. When you get inside someone's head, when you put yourself in their shoes, you can truly understand their actions. Maybe not understand them fully sometimes, but at least *empathize* with them.

As the years passed by, Adam fast realized a dark secret. A flip side to the coin his mom had introduced him to when he was being bullied by Mike Hart back when he was eight.

Nobody thought they were the bad guys.

In their own minds, everyone was doing the right thing.

And right now, knowing he was going to enjoy what awaited for Kyle Peters—what he was going to take away from him—he wasn't sure whether or not he was the good or the bad guy.

But he was going to do what he had to do anyway.

He got further up the stairs. The steps creaked beneath his feet. The closer he got to Ellicia's apartment, the more he could smell her perfume in the air. He knew her parents were away. He'd been sure to visit at a time when he had fewer people to get past and deal with.

It was just Ellicia, all alone.

Adam reached the top of the stairs. He wasn't sure how exactly Ellicia was going to fit into his plan just yet. But he knew that she would. He had ideas. Lots of ideas. And all of them involved getting to Kyle somehow.

He didn't want to be cruel to Ellicia, though.

It'd be much more satisfying to him if Ellicia joined his side by choice. That would hurt Kyle even more.

Not only would Adam have Kyle's abilities, but he'd have his girlfriend, too.

He walked further down the corridor towards Ellicia's room. He'd not always had such a downer on girls. He was a typical eighteen-year-old really. He'd had his relationships, most of which had fallen apart. He'd been betrayed one too many times. So that didn't exactly instill him with confidence.

But Ellicia was going to be different. Ellicia was going to be special.

He stood outside Ellicia's door and listened to the gentle sounds of her footsteps walking around in there. His hood was still up. He pulled it back, shuffled his dark locks around.

Then he took a deep breath and reached for the handle of the door.

"I'm through with him, Ellicia. I'm through with being afraid. And you should be too."

The guy's voice took Adam by surprise. He wasn't expecting Ellicia to have company.

"He's my boyfriend, Damon."

"And he's my best friend. Or at least he *was* my best friend, before all this... this..."

"He's just doing what he thinks is right."

"Don't make excuses for him, Ellicia. You were the one who said you were worried about him in the first place."

"I *am* worried about him. But that doesn't mean I'm turning my back on him."

Adam shuffled closer to the door. He heard a sigh.

"Kyle's made his bed. For the first time in his lazy life, he's actually made his bed. Now he has to lie in it."

"Damon, please."

"I'm sorry, Ellicia. It's been... it's been nice. Knowing you. Being friends with you. And I hope we'll stay friends for a long time. But you should see sense while you can and get far, far away from Kyle. He's dangerous. He's going to get us all in trouble. He's going to get us all killed."

Damon's footsteps got closer to the door.

Adam stepped back and leaned against the wall, trying to look as inconspicuous as possible.

"You really believe what the media are saying?" Ellicia asked.

"What about the media?"

"Adam. The people rising up. You really think that's the right thing? For the Resistance to have their powers taken away? I mean, for every mistake they make, they save ten more situations. We just hear the bad stuff because the news always tells us the bad stuff. But there's more to it than that. You know there is."

Damon didn't respond for a while. The silence stretched on, intense and unbearable.

Then, "Maybe Adam has a point. Maybe it is time someone else had a go at looking out for the world."

"You can't really think that."

"Well, I do."

Silence again.

Adam smiled.

"I'm sorry, Ellicia. Really. I... I hope you find your way."

He opened the door and stepped out into the corridor.

Adam watched Damon walk away. He watched him walk towards the stairs, big rucksack on his back.

He watched him, and he smiled.

He didn't need Ellicia anymore. Not yet.

He had a better idea.

22

"So. What now, genius?" Ember asked.

I looked ahead. All around, Adam's followers surrounded us. Some of them had flames in their hands. Others, electricity. I could see the skin of one girl turning to a red brick-like texture.

"She stole my damned ability," Stone said.

The girl smiled. "Not quite. I'm tougher."

Stone tightened his fists. "Yeah we'll see about that."

I looked over at the women and men that were being forced to work in this place. They were lying flat on the floor. Some of them were praying. Others were just crying.

"We could make this nice and easy," a voice opposite said.

I turned and saw a short ginger guy walking towards us. He had spikes sticking out of his palms. He wouldn't be much to reckon with if he didn't have those spikes.

"We could, could we?" I asked.

The guy smiled. "We're all people here, after all," he said. "I'm James. This is Billie. You know what we all have in common?"

"Go on."

"You took someone away from us. Someone we care about."

I sensed the mood shifting then. I couldn't put my finger on what it was, but there was a distinct shift in the atmosphere. "Aren't you gonna get on with it and take us back to Adam?"

James laughed. So too did a few of the others. "Oh, Kyle. We aren't taking you back to Adam. We came here for you because you're all ours. Because we want to deal with you ourselves."

I realized what this was, then. These people had been given abilities, and they were betraying Adam already. "Not sure your leader'll approve of that too much."

"Let him disapprove," Billie, the girl beside him, said. "What matters more to us is that you suffer for what you did. For what you put us through."

They started to walk towards us then, surrounding us even more.

I put a hand back. Held it out. I had to teleport us away from here. Far away.

"Yeah. I get that might be important to you. But we've got bigger fish to fry right now."

I went to teleport us away when I snapped back into the compound and fell to the floor.

I held my winded stomach. I looked up and saw Billie smiling as she got closer.

"What's up?" she asked. "Can't quite find your way outta here?"

I wiped my mouth and tried to teleport away again.

But once again, I just bounced right back into the compound.

This time, James was standing right in front of me.

He swung that spiked hand at my face.

I dodged it, rolling onto my side and shooting into the air. My flight was unbalanced and wobbly. I felt like I was learning to fly for the first time all over again, and I knew it had to be something to do with those powers Billie had used to disorient me.

I felt something smack into my side. I spun around and saw three of Adam's followers floating opposite me, all of them with flames in their hands, all of them firing.

I swooped away from them and clumsily landed under them instead of above them. I dragged one of their legs down and threw them into the two beside them.

All around me, I saw the fighting unfolding now. I saw Stone cracking his fist into the metal exoskeleton of a girl, who stood her ground and punched right back. I saw Ember firing flames at a woman who just extinguished them with water right away. I saw Vortex's eyes rolling back into her skull, only for her to be knocked to her side and distracted every time she tried.

I was about to fly down and help her when I felt something around my neck.

I looked down and saw some thick, rubber tentacles wrapped around my throat. They were slimy and crusty on the surface. I tried to break free of them, kicking and attempting to teleport, but still my teleportation was weak.

"Feel bad?" a deep voice whispered in my ear as the battle rallied on below. "Feel bad watching your little army collapse?"

I couldn't accept that.

I couldn't let everything get taken away.

I had to fight.

I squeezed my eyes together then I slammed my hands against that tentacle.

I froze it. I kept on going and going, even though the tentacle was getting harder around my neck in the process.

I kept on going until it was completely solid.

"Sorry for this," I said.

Then I smashed the tentacle in pieces and hurtled towards Billie.

I knew I had to stop Billie. She was the one blocking my teleportation. She was down on the ground fighting off Ember and Vortex, as the rest of the Resistance tried to stave off enemies of their own.

I flew faster towards her, still a little wobbly.

Then I felt something pierce my stomach.

I looked down.

There was a spike right through my torso.

Blood dripped down from it.

I felt myself go weak and cold and I fell to the floor.

I landed on my back. I put my hands on my stomach. It was bleeding badly. I had to focus.

James stood over me, my blood dripping from one of the spikes on his palms. "Now we watch as your powers trickle away with your life," he said. "Now we watch you get what you deserved for hurting us. For hurting our families."

I poured all my energy into healing that wound on my stomach.

But James was lifting his spikes again.

He was pointing them at my legs.

I squeezed my eyes shut and put all my attention and a little more onto that wound.

Then I heard a thud.

I was half-expecting to open my eyes and see another two spikes through me.

Instead, I saw Ember crouching over James and holding him down.

And then I saw him fire three of those flames at Billie, knocking her down and loosening her grip on her power suppressing skills.

"Go!" Ember shouted. He was on the floor. He didn't look like he was moving anytime soon.

I shook my head. "I can't—"

The flares ignited on his hands. "You're more powerful than all of us. You're the one they're after. Just... just get out of here!"

I didn't want to get away.

I didn't want to disappear.

I didn't want another Roadrunner on my hands.

But before I had a chance to argue, I felt Stone grab hold of me and drag me away.

Ember was still inside.

He was totally surrounded.

23

After reluctantly teleporting us away, I felt myself being dragged higher into the sky and away from the Amazon rainforest by Stone and the rest of the Resistance.

I saw the compound below disappearing into the mass of trees. The humidity of the air dropped, and the breeze cooled me down right away. My stomach still wrecked from the goddamned *spike* I'd taken through it, but I was still here. I was still alive. I'd healed over, mostly.

But Ember...

"Teleport us outta here," Stone said. Beside him, I saw Vortex and the rest of the Resistance members. "While you still can."

I looked down at the Amazon rainforest below.

"Kyle? We need to get away before—"

"I can't," I said.

Stone groaned. "What do you mean you can't?"

I pointed down. "Ember. We can't leave him behind."

"We had this debate when Roadrunner got stuck in this

mess. We didn't want to leave her, but we had to make that call in the end."

"And I regret making that call," I said.

I looked at Cassie. Looked right into her eyes.

"Ember is one of us. We can't just give up on him. We can't just leave him to... to whatever down there. We have to fight for him."

Cassie opened her mouth to protest, like she always did.

Then she closed it. Nodded. "Kyle's right."

Vortex frowned. "What?"

"Yeah. What?" Stone echoed.

"Ember wouldn't leave us behind."

"You clearly don't goddamned know him as well as I do, then."

"We've made mistakes in the past," I said. "We've—we've done things we aren't proud of. But more than ever right now, I realize we need to hold onto who we really are. We're the Resistance. And we need each other more than ever before."

Vortex shook her head. "I hear you, Kyle. I really do hear you. But going down there isn't keeping us together. It's a suicide mission."

I swallowed a lump in my throat and looked below. "Then so be it."

I flew down toward the compound. I didn't feel comfortable about doing it alone. But I didn't want to be responsible for the loss of someone else.

All I saw these days was loss. I clearly had to change something.

"Wait."

I felt a hand touch my arm. When I turned, I saw it was Cassie.

She smiled at me.

"You don't have to come, sis."

She punched me playfully. "Yes. Yes I do. You're right. I know it's reckless, but you're right. We have to stay together. We have to *fight* together. And that starts now."

I glanced above at Stone and Vortex, who kept on hovering there, totally still.

Then I looked back at Cassie. "Let's go get Ember."

I activated my invisibility and so too did Cassie.

We flew down towards the compound.

The further we got towards the compound, the more the need to speak with Cassie grew.

"What's on your mind?"

Her voice startled me. I turned around. She was completely invisible, so I couldn't see her. "How do you know something's on my mind if you can't even see me?"

"Wait, you *can't* see me? Guess I'm more powerful than I thought."

I bit my lip and didn't say anything.

"Wait. That's what's on your mind, isn't it?"

"I just don't get why you don't embrace your abilities more," I said.

"Kyle, we've had this—"

"You're strong. Just as strong as Daniel and me, maybe stronger. But you're afraid. Afraid of teleporting. Afraid of using the powers like I do. Afraid of something going wrong."

Cassie was silent for a few seconds. Then, "When you've been through what I've been through, a little caution's natural, bro. Maybe I'll get to where you are, in time. Or maybe I won't. But I use just enough. To me, that's all that matters. Now come on. Let's go get Ember."

As we approached, I was surprised how quiet it seemed to have got. The humidity hit me again, and I started sweating right away. But I couldn't see anyone outside the compound.

And through the smashed glass of the roof, I couldn't see anyone inside either.

I landed right in the middle of it. I noticed the people being forced to work here were still here, crying. They looked more distressed than ever.

I looked around, being careful to stay totally invisible. "You see him?" I whispered, no idea of where Cassie was but safe in the knowledge that she was invisible too.

"There," she said.

It took me a moment, but eventually I saw exactly where Cassie was looking.

Ember was lying flat on his back. He was trying to spark up his flames, but they were simmering out without as much as a puff.

"Ember," I said.

I walked over to him.

"Go away," he said.

I stopped. Frowned. "What?"

His pained face stared up into my eyes. He struggled to breathe. "Go... go away. Bomb. Bomb."

I didn't clock what Ember was on about, as Cassie dropped her invisibility and walked closer to us. "What's he saying?"

Then I saw it.

I saw the little flashing light right underneath Ember.

I saw the wires.

My body tensed.

"We have to—!"

I didn't finish speaking.

An explosion blasted from below Ember's body.

[24]

I smacked my head against the side of the building, hard.

After that, for a short while, I wasn't aware of anything.

Consciousness hit me in the form of a thick smell of smoke. I was choking. The smoke was totally jet black all around me. I could taste it in the back of my throat, and I couldn't breathe.

I tried to move but my body felt totally broken. I couldn't see my legs, but I was pretty sure they were snapped in two. I closed my eyes and tried to heal them, but I hadn't felt this weak while in possession of my powers since... since... well, I wasn't sure since when.

I looked around the smoke. I couldn't hear anything for the ringing in my ears. All around me, I saw rubble.

Then my gut turned when I thought back to my last memory before that explosion.

I'd been with Cassie. We'd searched the place for Ember, but it'd seemed empty. The group of Adam's followers was gone.

Then we'd found Ember.

Only there'd been a bomb right underneath him.

And before I could do anything to stop it exploding, it'd blown to pieces.

I attempted to heal myself again. Tears rolled down my cheeks as I snapped my legs back into place. The pain was so intense that I was screaming at the top of my voice.

When I'd finally done, still weak as hell, I leaned back against the broken wall and let the smoke fill my lungs.

"You're not just gonna sit there, are you?"

I looked to my left.

Ember was right beside me.

"Ember?"

He half-smiled at me. His clothes were ripped and damaged. He was covered in cuts and bruises.

But he was alive. And he was all in one piece.

He held out a hand. "Come on. Let's get you to your feet and let's get out of here."

I grabbed Ember's hand and got back on my feet. Slowly but surely, the memories of what'd happened before the explosion—literally milliseconds before the explosion—flooded back.

I'd managed to drag Ember away.

I'd thrown him to the other side of the room.

Then I'd flown into Cassie and knocked her out of the way of the blast.

Then, the explosion had ripped through the compound.

Then...

"Cassie," I said.

Ember turned around. "What?"

"Cassie. She was in here. She came here to help."

"I don't see her anywhere."

"I'm not leaving her behind," I shouted.

"Whoa. Okay. I didn't suggest leaving her behind. But let's just... let's just take this one step at a time. Okay?"

I was about to start searching for Cassie when I saw a body on the ground in front of me.

It was the woman who'd been crying not long ago. She was lying on her back and staring up at me in total fear.

"Demon," she said, in Spanish, panting for every breath. "Demon!"

My skin went cold as I looked around and realized exactly what'd happened. Exactly what I'd been drawn into, again.

I'd been set up.

The bomb had been put in there *not* because they thought it'd kill me, but because they knew it would make me look even more reckless and dangerous all over again.

And I'd fallen for it. Again.

I wasn't sure how far back Adam's plan stretched. Maybe the group who'd come for their own vengeance were all part of the setup after all. One thing was for sure. Adam was powerful. And he was screwing with me. Big-time.

I just prayed to God my sister wasn't a victim of that screwing.

I looked around the broken rubble in hope that I'd find her. But everywhere I looked there was just no sign of her. I looked up through the smoke and saw the bright sky above. It seemed so far away. I wondered how Stone, Vortex, and the other Resistance members were getting on. I couldn't blame them for not coming down here. They'd been the ones with the bad feeling about this whole thing, after all. They hadn't fallen for the trap like I had.

"Kyle."

I looked around and I saw Ember standing right at the back of the compound.

I walked towards him. I wasn't sure where exactly he was looking at first.

Then I noticed he was looking outside.

I stood at the back of the compound and followed his gaze.

Outside, I saw loads of trees had fallen. Further in the distance, I saw a small village burning away, smoke rising from it. I heard crying. I knew this was what I'd done. This was what my recklessness had caused.

I'd been on the scene. That would get back to the media, somehow. They'd use it against me, that was for sure.

"This is bad," Ember said.

His words echoed my thoughts exactly. But despite all the chaos around me, I just felt totally cold. I saw the life I could be living right now if I'd never discovered my powers. I'd be at home, probably playing video games with Damon and Avi. Sure, I wouldn't have had the courage to approach Ellicia, and sure, I'd probably still be bullied and a weak little dude.

But I'd still have my mom.

I would be living a safe life without this kind of responsibility.

That said, if I wasn't here, then who would've stopped Saint?

Who would've defeated him?

Who would've prevented him brainwashing the planet?

I was the one who'd stood against him. I was the one who'd defeated him, together with my family.

I was the one with the responsibility.

I turned around and headed back into the compound.

Then, I saw Cassie lying there in the rubble.

Totally still.

[25]

I didn't know what to do when I saw Cassie lying there in the rubble.

I didn't know what to think, how to act.

All I knew was that I had to get to her, and I had to make sure she was okay.

"Cassie!"

I ran over to her as fast as I could. My legs were still painful after snapping in two. Sure, I'd managed to heal them, but try breaking your legs and healing them then telling me it wasn't painful.

I landed by her side, coughing back some of the smoke. Ember was somewhere behind me, but I didn't really have any sense of him right now. All that mattered was Cassie, as selfish as it sounded. All that mattered was that she was okay.

"Cassie."

I put my arms around her and felt the warmth of her body seep through. Her eyes were closed. She was battered and bruised, just like the rest of us. But she looked like she'd taken the brunt of more of the explosion than any of us.

I squeezed her limp body tighter and pulled her closer. I felt my tears trickling down. "Please, sis. Not now. Not after everything. Please."

I knew Cassie had healing abilities, like me. She was powerful. She didn't *believe* she was as powerful as me, but I knew if she really believed in herself that she could be.

But she'd been hit by the explosion before she'd had a chance to activate any of her shields or begin the healing process. Sure, it was possible to fight off wounds when you were unconscious. But Cassie looked in a deep state of unconsciousness right now.

Plus, she didn't have the confidence. She didn't have the belief.

She needed both right now, even in unconsciousness.

"We need to go, Kyle."

I heard Ember's voice and I didn't want to accept that we were giving up. "I can't let her go."

"Then bring her with us. But we need to get away from here right now. We're not safe here. We're lucky to even still be here in the first place."

I swallowed a lump in my throat and looked down at Cassie. She was out cold. Totally out cold. I couldn't even tell if she was breathing.

"Please," I said, holding her hand tighter. "Just... just, please. If you can hear me, come back. Don't give up. Please. You're strong. I told you how strong you were. You just have to hear me, sis. You have to believe me."

I closed my eyes and I saw images of the pair of us when we were younger. I saw us playing together. I saw the happy times we'd had, the times we'd shared.

Then I saw the jokes and the laughter we'd had since. I saw Cassie's smile. I saw the love between her and Dad when they were reunited. I saw myself introducing the sister I thought I'd lost so long ago to friends I never thought she'd meet.

I saw everything and I felt a warmth emitting from my body. A warmth transmitting towards Cassie.

A warmth—

A cough.

I opened my tearful eyes.

Cassie was coughing.

"Cassie!"

I extinguished the smoke around us so the air was cleaner. Then I held my sister even tighter.

"What—"

"It's okay," I said. "You're okay now. I've got you."

"My chest. It's..."

"It's okay," I said. "You don't have to worry. None of us do. Not anymore."

"Kyle, I think there's someone coming."

Cassie looked up at me with tearful eyes and smiled. "Thank you."

I stroked her hair out of her face. "I didn't do anything. You did it. You healed yourself."

"I—"

"Kyle," Ember repeated. "Seriously."

"You did it, Cassie. You're so much stronger than you think. You just have to keep on believing it."

"Kyle!"

I barely acknowledged Ember's voice. I wasn't sure whether to believe him at first. But then I saw the movement in the corners of my eyes, and I heard whoever was coming getting closer.

I felt the anger burning up inside. I felt my rage coming to the surface.

Cassie was alive, but Adam's followers had hurt her.

Adam's followers had tried to take everything away from me, again.

They'd taken my respect away, sure. They'd taken my standing with the public away.

But they weren't going to take my family away from me.

I stood up, activated my powers, and felt ice stretch right across my hands.

I spun around and got ready to fire.

"Whoah. Hold it. Hold it."

I narrowed my eyes and lowered my hands. "Stone?"

Stone grunted. Beside him, Vortex emerged. And behind them, a few other members of the Resistance. "Sorry for the nasty surprise. At least you three made it. Quite an ugly explosion ripped through this place, not gonna lie."

I nodded. "Guessing we're not in the good books of the South American people now?"

"We've never been in the good books. But yeah. We're in the worst book, that's for sure. The Chamber of Secrets."

"What?" Vortex asked. "The Chamber of Secrets was my favorite."

"Never had you down as a Potter guy, Stone," I said.

He grimaced and blushed.

I knew I had him cornered.

We stood together, the group of us, and we looked back at the burning building. We looked at the debris. We looked at the rubble. But most of all, as much as we didn't want to, we looked at the fallen people who were still inside the compound.

We went back in there. Pulled the survivors out. They cursed at us. Screamed at us. They did everything they could to get away from us.

The village in the distance wasn't much better, either. When we arrived, they booed us, even when we helped people out who were wounded or injured.

It felt like there was nothing we could do to win back our reputation. Not anymore.

We'd broken it. There was no fixing it.

This was who we were now.

After two hours of cleaning up, we hovered together above the woods. We looked down on the empty space where the trees of the Amazon had once stood so proudly, for so many years. We looked at the gutted remains of the fallen compound. We looked at the smoldering village, and the approaching helicopters, no doubt media, who were heading over here to tar the name of the Resistance even more, and turn more people from us and to Adam.

"What now?" Ember asked.

I took a deep breath.

I didn't have the answer. Not this time.

All I knew was that we were the enemy now. The people were angry.

And we were going to have to fight if we wanted to survive.

Damon had no idea how long he was going away for.
Only that he had to go away. And he had to get away fast.

He walked down Prospect Heights. Prospect Park was just up ahead. The evening rain lashed down on him, completely soaking him. The traffic flew by him. When he'd set off walking, he'd had no idea where exactly he was heading. But now he seemed to be heading in the direction of Coney Island. He had some family who lived in Coney Island. Maybe he'd stay with them for a while.

He wiped the rain from his eyes and kept on walking, rucksack draped over his back. Sure, he could've got the subway, and he probably would have to get a cab eventually, but right now he wanted nothing more than to keep on walking. He felt like walking was the only thing that could clear his mind right now.

And he needed to clear his mind because his entire world was falling apart.

He felt a lump right above his chest when he thought about Kyle. His best friend of so many years. They'd grown up together. They'd been by each other's sides time and time again.

Damon had been there for Kyle when times were rough. And as tough as Kyle thought Damon was, Kyle had kept him happy a lot of the time, too.

But now Kyle was gone.

He cleared his throat and lowered his head as he walked past some shady looking figures standing outside a 7-Eleven. Damon felt their eyes on him as he walked past. He hoped his size would be enough to deter them, even if he couldn't fight for shit.

He kept on walking, the group ignoring him. He looked up and saw the road stretching onwards. He knew he was still a couple hour walk from Coney Island. He knew some of these areas could be risky, too. There were active gangs around here, and he was a damned big guy to target. Besides, the last thing he wanted to do was spend a night homeless.

He hadn't told anyone he was leaving. He didn't want them to worry. And sure, if he went to stay with his Coney Island relatives, word would get back to his parents eventually. Yeah. A real flaw in his plan.

But as long as he kept a low profile and kept on going... maybe. Just maybe.

He didn't like the idea that he was turning his back on his best friend. He didn't like looking at it that way. After all, he knew Kyle had good intentions.

That said, it felt like those intentions were unraveling. It felt like Kyle's responsibilities were becoming too great for him to manage. It felt like the whole world was building up like a weight on Kyle's shoulders, and he just couldn't keep on carrying it anymore.

And Damon had tried to stay by Kyle's side. So too had Avi, and Ellicia.

But as much as they hated to admit it, Kyle had changed.

And he hadn't changed for the better.

He looked back down the sidewalk, right along the highway. He needed to find a taxi now. He waited a few minutes, then moved when he saw some more creepy looking dudes heading his way. He hid down an alley at the side of the road, waited for them to disappear before stepping back out.

Then he saw a cab.

He stuck out a thumb and ran towards it.

Then he slipped in the rain.

He fell face-flat on the sidewalk. He felt his face start to burn, and he tasted blood. When he lifted his head, the cab was pulling away.

And behind him, he heard laughing voices getting closer.

He looked back.

The group he'd passed before were heading his way. They were looking right at him. They were laughing.

Damon's heart pounded. He struggled back to his feet, read-justing his rucksack. He started to run away from them when he saw another group up ahead. The one who'd passed him just before.

They were walking toward him now.

And they didn't look happy.

Damon stood there feeling totally defenseless. How damned cruel it was that he didn't have the ability to fight off these bullies. Instead, Kyle had those abilities. But Kyle wasn't using them for good anymore. He was being chaotic with them. Reckless.

Damon looked over his shoulder, his knees shaking, and he prepared for whatever was coming for him.

Then a car screeched its tires right beside him.

A window rolled down. He couldn't see the guy in front properly, but they stuck a thumb out of the window. "Get in. Now."

Damon didn't hesitate.

He jumped in the back of the car and slammed the door shut.

The car accelerated to life, and the group of would-be attackers was left behind.

Damon almost gave them the Vs but figured now wasn't the best time.

He leaned back against the headrest. "Thank you. Seriously."

He still couldn't see the guy in the front of the car. "Those guys were gonna beat you up. Can't be doing with bullies."

"Right," Damon said. He waited a few seconds, watched as the cars passed by on the other side of the road. "Just Coney Island, please. Mermaid Avenue, by West 22nd."

"You're a brave man walking these streets alone at this time."

Damon shrugged. He hadn't been called "brave" all that often. "I guess I needed to clear my head."

"Hmm," the guy said. And Damon suddenly realized he probably shouldn't be letting this guy in on his problems. And also that he shouldn't have jumped into the back of his car in the first place. But hey. He was being chased. This guy had offered him a ride. It seemed like the only option he had at the time.

They drove for about fifteen minutes. Every time Damon spoke, the driver either grunted, or replied with a really short answer. He didn't seem to be one for small talk.

After twenty minutes driving and no sign of the coast, Damon started to worry.

"Umm, this is Bellaire, right?"

"Right."

"Coney Island? That's where I... Hey, man, I think I'll get out and..."

He saw the man's eyes in the rearview mirror then. Piercing. Green. But from what he could make out of his face, he was younger than he'd thought. "We're not going to Coney Island, Damon."

Damon felt his stomach turn. He reached for the back door with his clammy hand, but the car was moving too fast for him to even think about jumping out. "How... how do you know my name?"

The guy turned away from the driver's seat and the steering wheel. He looked right into Damon's eyes.

It took Damon a few seconds to realize exactly who it was.

But when he did, he felt totally cold inside.

"I'm Adam," he said. "And I think you can help bring your best friend back down to earth."

27

Three days in the middle of Greenland and I was hating it already.

Apparently, it was the middle of the day, but the sky didn't really tell that story. The clouds were thick and black, and the rain was constant. We were literally in the middle of nowhere. Every now and then, I'd take visits to shops around the world for food, but it wasn't exactly a luxury way of life. Once again, not for the first time in its existence, The Resistance was on the run. Only this time it was on the run from the very people it'd sworn to protect.

I looked ahead at the vast expanse of wilderness. Greenland was a nice country, geographically stunning, but it wasn't exactly paradise. Damon would be in his element here, though. He was into his rocks and things like that. I missed Damon, and I wished he was here. I wished Avi was here. I wished Dad and Ellicia were here.

Life was different. I'd grown so distant from them without even realizing. It hurt.

I heard footsteps on the creaky floorboards of the cabin we were staying outside. It was some kind of old fishing cabin, apparently, but I couldn't see any lakes nearby, unless it'd frozen over completely.

When I turned around, I saw Cassie looking at me.

I sighed, then looked back out the window. "Come to gloat?"

"Kyle," Cassie said, tutting. She put a hand on my arm. "You've gotta snap out of this. It's not doing you or anyone good."

"I'm starting to see it now. Starting to see what I've done."

"What you've done?"

"The recklessness. Or whatever you want to call it. I just... I thought I was doing the right thing. But I wasn't. Now I see that. And now we're all in here hiding because the people have just decided enough's enough."

Cassie stood by my side. We were both silent. I could tell she was deep in thought. I didn't want to ask her what she was thinking about because I didn't want to risk it being another reminder of all the bad crap I'd done, etcetera etcetera etcetera.

"We have to fight back against him," I said. I wasn't sure where the words came from. They just kind of blurted out of nowhere.

Cassie looked at me now. She was frowning. "What?"

"Adam. We need to take the fight back to him."

She had such a look of pity on her face. She tilted her head, then shook it.

"What?" I said.

"It doesn't matter."

"No, it matters. Tell me."

"I just think you're living a pipe dream if you think we can defeat Adam when he's got the whole world behind him."

A bitter taste filled my mouth. There was such defeat in Cassie's voice. I looked away and took some deep breaths of the biting cold air outside. I didn't want to accept Cassie was right. But she had a point.

"Our own people have turned on us," she said. "They've decided they don't like our methods."

"My methods."

"*Our* methods," Cassie said. She squeezed my arm a little tighter. "And when the people speak, it's hard to turn against their wishes. You can only force so much respect. Look at Saint. And look where it got him. If we fight back, we *are* Saint. We are just ULTRAs upset that the power's been taken away from us when really, we have no right to be."

I shook my head. In truth, I had mixed emotions about what Cassie was saying. She had a point. But there was something about Adam that worried me. I couldn't believe he was acting entirely in humanity's best interests. There had to be something in it for him.

"So this is what I suggest," Cassie said. "We go back in the main room with the rest of our team, and we work out a way we're gonna lay low and re-integrate with the world."

"Re-integrate with the world?"

Cassie couldn't look me in the eye. "I... I don't like saying this. But I can't see any other way. I'm sorry."

She let go of my arm and walked back to the main room, where Ember, Stone, and Vortex were waiting.

"Maybe we don't have to force their respect," I said.

Cassie stopped. She turned around. "Huh?"

"Humanity. Maybe we don't have to force their respect. Maybe... maybe we fight our way back by proving we're the right ones to watch over this world. By proving we're more trust-worthy than Adam."

Cassie smiled. She started to open her lips.

Then a massive bang crashed against the roof of the cabin.

28

I sparked my abilities the second I heard the bang against the roof.

But I didn't have much chance to do anything about them.

The roof caved in. Through it, fell two people. I knew they had to be Adam's followers. They were here for us.

I lifted my hands and got ready to blast a load of ice at the intruders. If we were running, then I couldn't hold back anymore. I didn't care who they were. I didn't care where they came from. I just had to...

When I regained my focus, it dawned on me exactly who it was.

Daniel Septer stood right opposite me. Behind him, there was a girl I also recognized.

I lifted my hands and pointed them at her.

It was Chaos. The ULTRA who had baited me to the middle of the Kenyan mall and brought on that explosion.

"Wait," Daniel said.

He lifted his hands in front of Chaos. All of us stood around now, braced to use our abilities against the intruders if we needed to.

"What is this?" I asked.

Daniel smiled. "You always have the best kind of welcome parties, brother. Always roll out the red carpet treatment for me."

"You can forgive us for being a little touchy," Ember said. "We're all being hunted down, after all."

"And aren't *you* one of Adam's?" Stone grunted, glaring at Chaos.

She shook her head and tutted. She didn't look totally confident or comfortable. Definitely not as much as she had when I'd last encountered her.

"Why are you here?" I asked.

"Lower your hands."

"I'm not—"

"We're all on the same side here, Kyle. Everyone. We're all fighting for the same cause."

"That's strange," Stone said. "We haven't seen you in a long, long time. Jumping ship?"

"Look," Daniel said, staying as composed as possible. "We can't have a decent, honest conversation if we've all got our powers charged up and ready to fire. So please. Follow my lead. Lower your hands. Everyone."

I looked around the room to gauge the mood. I got a sense that nobody was keen on a fight right now. There wasn't exactly an appetite for one.

I lowered my hands, and the rest of the Resistance followed my lead.

"That's better," Daniel said. "Much prefer the chilled out vibe."

"You still haven't answered my question. What are you doing here? And what is *she* doing here?"

Daniel frowned, then turned to Chaos. "I'm sorry. He's never been a charmer, my brother."

Chaos grinned at me. "It's cool. I've met kids like him many times. All talk when they're hiding behind their powers, but without them, well... We all know what we are without our powers."

"You're not exactly making us wanna shake hands with you right now," Stone said.

"Just quit it, okay?" I said. "All of you. Just quit it. Daniel. What are you doing here?"

Daniel took a deep breath, clearly enjoying how uptight we all were, then he walked around the debris of the broken cabin roof, slowly. "While you've been hiding in the middle of Greenland—and not hiding very well—I've actually been out there doing things."

"Doing things?"

"Taking responsibility. Trying to figure out ways to stop Adam. That's where I met Chaos."

He held out his hands like he was turning the spotlight on her.

"And what does Chaos have to do with anything?" Vortex asked.

"He took my powers away," Chaos said.

Everyone turned to look at her. Her voice sounded more cracked and uncertain than I expected.

"Adam did?" I asked. "Why would he do that?"

"He isn't interested in redistributing power to the people. All he's interested in is claiming more power for himself. Really, he's just keen on toppling order. He'll convert so many humans, then he'll just drop the rest of the population. He wants to be worshiped, and he wants to lead. Nothing else."

"And why should we trust you?" Cassie asked.

"You don't have to trust me. I get why you wouldn't. What

happened back in Kenya was screwy, but even I didn't know Adam planted a bomb there."

"Bullshit," I said. "You tricked me. You made it look like I caused that explosion."

"I just followed Adam's command, word by word. I didn't know what would happen. I knew we were framing you somehow, but that's all he told me. I wouldn't have gone ahead if I'd known... if I'd known."

"Well, what's done's done. There's no going back."

"No, there isn't," Chaos said.

"What makes you so sure you know Adam so well anyway?"

"We dated, for a while."

"You dated *him*?"

"I was going through a rough patch after my sister got killed in an ULTRA battle. I guess I saw something in him, and he made me feel like he saw something in me. I got transfixed. Maybe I was obsessed. So obsessed that I didn't see what he was doing, not for real. Not until it was too late."

She looked down at the floor, and I sensed sadness in her. An air of total regret.

"He has a way of making you feel like you're the most wanted person in the world. Of making you feel... feel special. But now I see him doing the same thing to everyone else. I see him using the same tricks on the people that follow him. And I know now I'm not special. Not to him. I was just a part of his game."

Part of me was hesitant. Part of me remembered what Cassie said about not being able to force respect. But right now, I knew we were the ones to lead this world. We were the ones who could look out for people's best interests. Sure, we wanted power, but we wanted it for good reasons.

"But there's a way to stop Adam before he converts any more people.

"How?"

"Adam isn't an ULTRA," Cassie said.

I frowned. "What?"

"Adam isn't an ULTRA. He's just a regular guy. A regular weak guy."

"Then how does he take abilities? How does he hand them out?"

"He wears a glove."

The room went silent.

Stone broke the quiet. "A glove?"

"I think it's government tech. He didn't tell me how he got it and where, but he claims he stole it when the world went to crap last year. When Adam wears it, he gains the ability to take powers from other ULTRAs and pass them on. There's a slight buffer, and he can use the abilities of those he's absorbed for a short time even if he commits to passing them on; otherwise, he's stuck with them."

"Then why doesn't he just keep them all?"

"It doesn't seem to work like that," Chaos said. "He has a choice. One ULTRA's abilities to keep at one time. If he passes the power on, he loses those abilities himself. And it isn't going to totally shock you to find out which ULTRA's abilities he wants to keep."

I saw everyone's eyes turn on me. "Mine."

"We take that glove away from him, and we make him totally powerless."

"And the rest of the people around him? 'Cause it's his army that's really strong."

"We try to win them over. If we don't, well. We have a glove. We can use it to take those powers away and return them to their original owners."

"It's impossible," I said.

"Maybe so. But if we don't try getting that glove from Adam, eventually, he's going to get to you. Then he's going to be more powerful than you. And trust me, I ain't your biggest fan, but I'd much rather a wimp like you had your abilities than a psychopath like Adam."

"Thanks, I guess?"

"Take it. It's the only compliment you're gonna get."

"And how the hell are we going to take that glove away from Adam?"

Chaos tilted her head to one side. "He goes to a nightclub in Tokyo every Friday."

"Course he does," I said.

"He likes to go there to just be himself all over again. To be a normal eighteen-year-old. He doesn't wear the glove when he's there. He rents a room above the place. He keeps the glove in there when he's at the bar."

"How do you know this?"

Chaos lifted an eyebrow. "You really wanna know all the things I've seen in that room with Adam?"

I felt my throat tighten and turned away. "Oh."

"Yeah. Didn't think so."

A smile flickered at the corner of Chaos' mouth. She looked around.

"I can get in there and meet with Adam. I can tell him I've seen the way forward. And while I'm chatting with him, Kyle can sneak upstairs and take that glove. But you have to be careful. He does have his followers with him now. One of them might be able to tell when powers are being used. So you need to show real caution."

I nodded, scratching the back of my neck. It sounded pretty straightforward, which worried me because the straightforward plans were usually the ones to be cautious about.

"So are you in?" Chaos asked.

I looked around at the Resistance. I didn't know what to say. It was forceful. It was against the will of the people.

But sometimes, responsibility forced you to make the uncomfortable decisions for other people that might not seem in their best interests at the time.

"We'll do it," I said. "We'll help you. And we'll go get that glove."

The rest of the Resistance nodded. Cassie was a little more hesitant, but eventually, she agreed too.

We were taking the fight to Adam.

We were finishing his reign.

"Damn," Stone said. "All this drama and all this loss, and the fate of the planet rests on a goddamned mitten."

29

Damon looked in the cracked mirror inside the public restroom and he couldn't stop his hand shaking.

It was totally pitch black outside. He could hear voices every now and then, but he barely even acknowledged them. They didn't mean anything to him. Not compared to what he was focused on. Not compared to what his mind and his energy were totally surrounded by.

He looked down at his hands. They were shaking completely. He could feel tears building behind his eyes, and he couldn't taste a thing but sick. He'd been pretty hungry when he set off walking away from Staten Island. Now, the thought of food disgusted and nauseated him.

He knew exactly why.

He just didn't like revisiting the memory of what happened in the car.

What happened when Adam turned around and faced him.

He reached down into the sink and stuck his hands under the tap. When they were full, he covered his face with water. But the water felt slimy, and he didn't feel any better for trying to refresh himself.

Instead, he just felt afraid.

Totally afraid.

This wasn't the life he'd signed up for. This wasn't the life he'd agreed to.

He splashed some more water on his face as the memories flooded back into his mind, unavoidable.

Someone picking him up and helping bail him out against those people following him.

Jumping into the car and realizing it was Adam.

Adam turning around, telling Damon he knew a way to deal with Kyle. To bring him back down to earth.

As much as Damon didn't want to talk about Kyle behind his back with anyone, let alone Adam, he'd heard what Adam said. He'd heard it loud and clear.

But he still hadn't agreed to *this*.

He pulled his face up from the sink.

He saw a man standing at the back of the cubicle.

He had his hood pulled up over his eyes, and he was holding a knife.

Damon felt that instinctive terror kick in.

"Your phone and your wallet. Don't screw around with me, kid."

He gestured for Damon to move toward him. And a part of Damon wanted to comply. He didn't want any trouble. He'd never liked trouble. He just wanted to get this done with and get out of here.

"Right now. Do it, or I swear I'll shoot you in your fat little belly."

Damon looked over at the restroom door. Tried to figure out how quickly he could get there and get out.

"Please," Damon said. "I don't want any—"

The guy ran at Damon and pressed him back against the

wall. He pushed the gun right between Damon's eyes. "You hand over your shit or I'll take your shit away myself. And you don't want that, man. You don't want that at all. So how we gonna do this?"

Damon felt a tear rolling down his face as the guy breathed sour breath at him. "You really shouldn't have done that."

The mugger's face turned. "What—"

Damon pressed his hand against the mugger's head.

Sparks of electricity ignited from his fingertips.

The man started to scream.

Damon kept on holding his head, unable to let go. He shouted out himself. The pain of the electricity was too intense. His blood was boiling. Every single hair on his body felt like it was being pulled at, slowly. He felt like he was going to explode.

Then the guy dropped to his knees and the electricity stopped.

Damon looked at the smoking body of the guy. His eyes were closed. He didn't look like he would be getting back to his feet anytime soon.

Then he looked down at his hands.

Then back into the mirror.

He knew what he was now. He knew what Adam had turned him into.

And he knew what Adam wanted him to do.

What the *people* wanted to do.

He swallowed another bout of sick as he thought about Kyle, his best friend, and all the rough times they'd been through together.

Then he thought of the chaos and destruction Kyle was causing, how the power was getting to his head and he couldn't see the truth anymore, and he knew that as hard as it was going to be, he was going to have to do something about it.

Damon looked back at his hands.

Electricity sparked across his fingertips.

He took a deep breath and walked over the paralyzed body of the guy, out of the public restroom and into the wind.

He knew what he had to do.

30

My first trip to a Tokyo nightclub wasn't exactly in the circumstances I'd hoped.

The night sky was pitch black, but you could easily be fooled into thinking it was the middle of the day, the neon lights were so bright. The street was one of the loudest I'd ever come across. Everywhere, people bustled past one another, the smell of sweat intense and the taste of alcohol strong. It was as if, to these people, nothing major was happening in the world at all. Like there was nothing going on with the ULTRAs, or that Adam even existed.

All that mattered to these people right now was that they were out to party, and nothing was going to get in their way.

I was here for a different reason.

"It's important that you just stick with me," Chaos said. She had a hood pulled right over her head. "If you do that, they'll let you in."

"You're not old enough to get in this place, surely?"

"It's about who you know. Anyway. Stand tall and look tough. Here we go."

"Can't I just—"

"No. We do this the proper way. You use your powers and Adam will figure out you're here."

"One of the perks of the glove?"

"Something like that."

Chaos cleared her throat, then she and I approached the entrance to the club, towards the security guards.

We were here because Chaos claimed she'd managed to reach out to Adam. She'd had her powers taken away, but she'd told him that she could get to me and prove her allegiance. It was risky, and I hoped she wasn't double-crossing me. But she insisted she came here because she knew Adam liked a drink here—again, he wasn't legal—the drinking age was twenty in Japan—but he had his ways.

But also because Adam left that glove of his in his room above the club whenever he visited here.

"You sure he's not gonna be wearing his glove?" I asked.

Chaos nodded. "Look, I've been here a ton of times with Adam. I swear. He never wears that glove when he's here."

"Maybe things have changed since you two last hung out, though."

"Like?"

"Like, I dunno, him taking all your powers away?"

"Even more reason to give his arm a rest from the glove then, huh?"

I saw Chaos smile. I didn't want to put all my faith in her. Doing so felt dangerous.

But right now, I knew I had no choice but to trust her.

Or at least try.

"Just get inside. Wait for me to start talking with Adam. When I do, give it five minutes, then make your move."

"And if I don't get in?"

"You will."

I saw the bouncer lift a hand when Chaos approached. She lifted her head and looked right up at him.

After a few seconds, he nodded, and Chaos walked inside.

I held my breath, my throat tightening, and I walked right after Chaos.

The bouncer lifted his arm.

He was a tall, bulky man with a stare that could break glass.

"I'm with—"

"No," he said.

I looked for Chaos, but she'd already disappeared out of sight into the bright lights and blasting music of the club. "Did she not—"

"Too young. Go. Now."

I thought about skipping past his arms, using my powers to teleport inside. See how tough they were then.

But then I knew causing a scene was a terrible idea. It'd make Adam realize there was something amiss.

Sensing the crowd behind getting agitated to get inside, I sighed and turned away.

I stood outside, back against the wall. The longer time stretched on, the more agitated I got. Was Chaos with Adam now?

I looked over my shoulder. I remembered what our plan was. Chaos would go in there, meet with Adam, and then I'd wait until the pair were together before sneaking upstairs and getting the glove.

But I was outside, and I couldn't see whether they were together right now.

I had to get inside.

I had to risk it.

I had to know whether now was the time.

I closed my eyes, held my breath, and activated my invisibility.

Then I disappeared behind the wall and emerged inside the nightclub.

The music and lights were even louder and brighter in here, even more head-spinning. I looked around. I couldn't see Chaos anywhere or Adam. But I felt disoriented. My head was spinning.

If I couldn't see them, then where were they?

I walked towards the back of the nightclub. Every step was sluggish and forced. I nearly bumped into a few people on my way. My invisibility felt like it was simmering. What was happening to me? Why did I feel so weak?

Something was wrong. It had to be wrong.

But I didn't have any time at all to dwell on it right now.

I searched the bar area even further for Chaos and Adam. Still no sign of them. I scanned the place twice, three times, four times, but again, still no sign of them.

Then I saw the stairs leading up to the next level of the nightclub.

My stomach turned. I knew that up there, I'd find Adam's room. The room where he kept the glove. The glove that took abilities away and gave him all his power and control. If I got up there, I could do my job and take the glove away.

But where was Chaos?

I looked over my shoulder once more. It felt like the people in the club were looking at me. But they couldn't be. I was just being paranoid. I was invisible, so they couldn't see a thing.

I turned around, took a deep breath and went to climb the stairs.

I wasn't sure what made me turn around. Call it instinct. Call it a sixth sense. Call it whatever you want.

But I did turn around.

And I was glad I did.

At the front of the nightclub, I saw five, six, seven, eight shady looking characters dressed all in black walk inside.

And although I was invisible, I didn't just *feel* like they were looking right at me.

I was convinced they were looking right at me.

31

Chaos didn't see Adam anywhere.

She looked over her shoulder. She knew Kyle was supposed to be right behind her. But now, there was no sign of him. Typical guy. Must've fumbled his lines upon entry.

But still. If he'd told the bouncers he was with her, then they'd have let him inside. She was certain of it.

Maybe Adam really had changed since their last meeting after all.

She kept her head down, eager not to draw any attention to herself. She'd been here so many times, but now, it felt different. It felt like the eyes were all on her even though she knew she was just being paranoid. Her paranoia wasn't totally without meaning, though. Last time she'd been here, Adam had planted some of his followers on guard, filled the place with them. So if she was a bit paranoid, surely it's excusable.

She searched the lower floor, squinting into the strobe lights and over at the bar where she'd met Adam several times before. But he was nowhere to be seen. That was strange. She'd reached out to him. He'd got back to her and told her he liked her idea of putting the past behind them. He even promised to give her some powers of her own all over again if they could see eye to eye.

And it was tempting. It was so tempting.

But she worried about Adam. He seemed dangerous.

She didn't trust him anymore.

She looked back over her shoulder. Still no sign of Kyle. She hoped he was okay out there. Well, he must be. He could fight. And if he fought, there'd be a scene right now. Which meant that he was waiting outside, figuring out how to progress. She hoped he didn't do anything rash like use his powers. She knew Adam had people that were especially perceptive when it came to picking out powers.

She cleared her throat and smiled at someone as she passed by them. The guy smiled back at her. He was a lot older, and his teeth were too white and shiny to be trusted. He gave her the creeps.

She walked over to the stairs that led up to Adam's room. She knew that if Adam was here, the glove that gave him all his powers would be up there. Sure, part of the plan was for Kyle to take that glove. But maybe he wouldn't have to.

A ton of scenarios ran through Chaos' mind. Maybe Adam was in the bathroom. Which meant she had to hurry because he wouldn't be there long.

Or maybe he was up there waiting for her. Maybe this was a trap.

She looked over her shoulder. No. This wasn't a trap. Adam just wasn't here yet.

She had to make her move while she had the chance.

She started to climb the stairs.

The further she got, the more worried she grew about what she was doing. This was madness. She was walking right into trouble. Adam was clever, so she had to be careful.

But what wrong was she doing, really? She was just walking to his room. How wrong was that?

She reached the top of the steps and looked right down to the corridor towards Adam's room.

Her heart pounded. Every instinct in her body told her to turn around and back away. This wasn't right. Something was deadly wrong.

But she walked regardless.

She heard the muffled music from below, and it creeped her out how much the peace and quiet contrasted with the noise. She didn't want to stick around here long. She wanted to check that room then leave, glove or no glove.

She was risking everything right now. And she didn't even know if Kyle was safe or not.

She walked a little quicker towards the room.

She saw a shadow up ahead.

She stopped. Completely froze in the middle of the corridor. She'd seen movement. No doubt about it. It'd moved across the corridor so quickly, then disappeared.

She opened her mouth to say something, then realized that was just reckless. She had to stay quiet. Had to keep a low profile.

She hadn't seen anyone or anything. She can't have.

She walked right up to Adam's door and stood in front of it.

She put her hands against it. She closed her eyes and tried to listen beyond it. If only she had her powers, she wouldn't feel so weak.

If she got the glove, she could have powers again.

She could take her powers back from whoever Adam had given them to.

She could be *herself* again.

Her hands shook as she moved them down to the door handle. For a moment, she felt a sobering wave of realization.

She'd need a keycard. She'd have to go downstairs and steal one.

Then she saw the door was already partly open.

She was still again for a few moments. Quiet, as she tried to get her head around what was going on.

She looked to her left and right. Screw it. She'd made it this far. She wasn't giving up now.

She pushed open the door.

The room was empty, but the lights above the double bed were on. There was a clinical vibe about the room like it was soulless.

But Chaos didn't dwell on that.

Not when she saw what was sitting right on top of the bed.

She walked into the room towards the metal box. She knew what was in there. She'd seen it so many times already.

Adam's glove.

She looked around the room as she rushed toward the bed. She was still alone. Still totally alone.

She reached the bed. Held her breath. The glove had to be here. It just had to be.

To Chaos' delight and relief, it was.

She felt a smile stretch across her face.

Then she heard footsteps behind.

The hairs on the back of her neck stood on end. She didn't want to turn around because she didn't want to see who or what was there.

But she knew exactly who it was already.

So she turned around.

Adam stood right by his door, smiling.

Behind him, a man and a woman.

Both of them were clearly his followers.

He lifted a hand. Pointed at the box. "Go on. Take it. Keep it as a souvenir."

Chaos didn't move for a second. She shook all over, sure, and her heart was rapid, absolutely. But she didn't move, like a rabbit caught in the headlights of Adam's charming, bright green eyes.

Then she lunged into the box.

She fumbled to get the glove on. She tried to drag it over her arm.

She had to get it on.

She had to use it before Adam got to her.

She turned. Pointed it at Adam, and the two people beside him.

And then...

32

I knew the guys entering the club were looking right at me even though my invisibility was activated, and I knew damned well that I was in for a fight, whether I liked it or not.

I could do with a good, unfair fight stacked in my favor. But I was feeling sluggish for some reason, like something was suffocating my powers. So I hoped I wouldn't have to get into a fight.

But yeah. The guys at the door now—twenty of them—lifted their hands.

Flames emerged from the palms of some.

Electricity from others.

They were all looking right at me and getting ready to fire.

Didn't look like I was off the hook this time.

They fired at me.

I flew to my right, out of the way of the initial blast. I didn't land as smoothly as I'd have liked, cracking the right side of my body against a table. A man and a woman were sat around it having drinks. Both of them screamed when I landed in front of them, the guy a bit louder than the woman.

I jumped back up and was face to face with a muscular man with a padded black outfit.

I pulled back my fist and punched him, but he knocked it away.

I kicked at him.

He swooped his arm toward my legs, trying to knock me from the table.

I jumped up, teleported right behind him, then grabbed his back and lifted him.

I turned around and threw him across the club, over into three of his friends, who were charging up and getting ready to fire at me.

The electricity hit their friend as he hit them, and they fell down like dominoes.

I ran along the wall to dodge the small spray of gunfire which came from the hands of another of Adam's followers. The club was in chaos now. Everyone was screaming, battling to get out. I kept on moving against the wall. Then I jumped up and elbowed a guy right in the head.

Again, though, my landing was sluggish, and before I knew it I was lying on the floor surrounded by six of Adam's followers.

All of them had their powers activated.

All of them got ready to fire.

I spun around on my back and made a tiny wormhole appear underneath all of their feet.

Then I clapped my hands together.

They fell down through the floor, like it'd crumbled away beneath their feet.

I closed the wormhole then I jumped back up.

There were just four of them left now.

But they had hostages.

I felt anger building up. I tensed my fists. Taking hostages was weak. It was a total coward's game. I wasn't going to leave these people behind. I wasn't going to let them die.

I looked at the four men standing with their hostages, all of them one each, all of them on their knees.

I ground my teeth together, and felt the floor shake. I saw lights sparking, and I felt like time was slowing down.

I closed my eyes.

Took a deep breath.

Then I fired at the hostages.

They disappeared, dragged away from the club and through a wormhole.

Only I'd sent them somewhere safe.

Now it was just me, face to face with the remaining four ULTRAs.

I started to power up when I heard more footsteps outside, and saw more ULTRAs running in. Dammit. There were more of them. I had to check on Adam's room upstairs. I hadn't seen Chaos in a long time. I had to know she was okay.

I thought about fighting off the rest of these ULTRAs. No doubt I had the ability to. But I just didn't know if I had the *time* to.

So I shot over to the other side of the club.

I transported my way up the stairs, as the fire of the remaining ULTRAs sounded out behind me.

I ran over to the third door on the right, which Chaos told me was Adam's.

It was already open wide.

I ran inside.

There was nobody in the room.

Just a box on the bed.

A box, which Chaos said contained the glove.

I heard the footsteps getting closer and I knew I didn't have long left.

I rushed over to the bed, my powers still a little shaky for some reason. Must be an ULTRA who had the ability to weaken the powers of others.

I opened the box.

When I saw what was inside, my body went totally cold, and I felt vomit fill my mouth.

I heard the footsteps reach the door and I knew Adam was here for me. I knew this was all some kind of trap.

And as much as I knew I needed to fight, I knew I couldn't. Not right now.

I teleported myself away before they could catch me.

But as I disappeared, I couldn't get what I'd seen out of my aching head.

The glove wasn't in the box.

Instead, Chaos' head was in the box.

And next to her head, a little note written in blood.

Too late.

33

Damon watched the news unfolding about his best friend and his latest mishap.

This time, there was a showdown at a nightclub in the middle of Tokyo. Not only had it left an ULTRA dead, but it had left several security guards wounded, too. It was unconfirmed whether anyone else had died. No doubt more reports would emerge in time.

But the amount of chaotic confrontations Kyle was getting himself dragged into was unsettling Damon.

He wanted to bring his best friend back down to earth.

He wanted Kyle back.

He rolled over in his bed and squeezed his eyes shut. He was tired, and he had no appetite. Downstairs, he could hear his parents' television, and he could hear rain rattling against his window. He just wanted to keep his eyes closed and forget about everything. He didn't want to be a part of all this anymore.

But he had powers, now. He had been given abilities by Adam. The ability to paralyze people and ULTRAs. And he'd been given a responsibility that he was genuinely starting to believe would benefit the world, too.

He had to bring Kyle to his knees, and then Adam could take his powers away from him.

He thought about approaching Kyle directly. Working something out between them. Getting him to disappear so Damon didn't have to do a thing, and Adam would never find him.

But Damon knew damn well Kyle wasn't going to listen to him. Not now he was "Glacies". Not anymore.

There was no glossing over the facts. They were on the news. They were in the anger of the people on the streets.

Kyle was not just hurting himself.

He was hurting other people.

That had to stop.

He lifted his phone and hovered over Ellicia's name. He didn't like this method. He didn't want to take this approach. But he needed to do something radical, and if Kyle listened to anyone, it would be Ellicia.

He tapped on her name and held his breath.

He listened to the dialing tone and waited for her to answer.

After six rings, he went to cancel the call. No. He had to go about this another way. He couldn't scheme and go behind Kyle's back. He had to—

"Damon?"

Damon heard Ellicia's voice and his mouth went dry.

"You there?"

"Yeah, I..."

"Are you okay?"

Damon tensed his eyes shut and squeezed the bridge of his nose. The sickness in his body intensified. "Ellicia, I—I need you to get in touch with Kyle."

"What's going on?"

"I need his help. Desperately. Please."

"Damon? Are you—"

Damon canceled the call.

He threw his phone across the room.

When he looked down at his hands, he saw electricity tingling across them.

Now, he just had to wait.

34

"Ahead in a box. You've got to give the guy credit. That's some Grade-A *Se7en* level shit."

I was in the Lake District, England, with Daniel and Cassie. It was dark. And cold. And rainy. Yeah, all the stereotypes about Britain were true after all. We were right at the top of one of the highest hills. It felt like we were in the middle of nowhere, looking down at the mass of trees and the tiny villages in the distance, barely a speck on the landscape. And that was just how we wanted it right now.

The discovery of Chaos had left us all shaken.

The rest of the Resistance had gone AWOL. I couldn't blame them, really. They were being hunted down by Adam and his followers. And as much as I could do with all the support I could get right now, they all had problems of their own. They all had *lives* of their own.

I had to let them fight their own battles.

I knew they'd be here for me in time when I really needed them.

At least I hoped so.

I listened to the breeze and smelled the fresh pine in the distance. I hadn't spoken for a long time. That's because I couldn't stop thinking. Thinking of what to do next. Of how we had to progress.

"I mean, the glove's gone," Daniel said, echoing my thoughts. "And we know now that Adam ain't too kind to his exes. So he's hardly gonna give up without a fight."

"We take the fight to him. Directly. To him and his people."

Cassie tutted. "And how do we do that?"

I opened my mouth. I truly didn't have an answer.

But I had to try.

"Whatever happens, we know for a fact that we have to take on Adam and his people."

"You keep saying that," Daniel said, crunching down on an apple. "Not a real plan."

"We're strong, the three of us."

"But we still need a plan," Cassie said.

I sighed and nodded. Why couldn't it just be as easy as the three of us forcing our way to Adam through his mass of ULTRAs and take him down?

"I appreciate what you want to do," Cassie said. "But to get to Adam, we have to get through his followers. And they won't go down without a fight. And fighting them... well, Adam's framed that as us fighting the people."

"I say we mow them down anyway," Daniel said. "They've picked their side. Let them pay for it."

Cassie shook her head. "No. You know how we work. We don't kill our own."

"They're not our own," Daniel said. "They're power-mad idiots that've been gifted their abilities by an even bigger power-mad idiot."

"But they're still people," Cassie said.

We were quiet again for some time. Then eventually, I found myself speaking, out of nowhere, as if someone was speaking through me.

"The people might not want us to win right now. We might look like the bad guys for even fighting Adam. But in the long run, we'll go down in history as having done the right thing."

"What's that supposed to mean?" Cassie asked.

I stood up. Took a deep breath of the damp air. Then I turned back round to face my biological brother and sister. "We're going to find a way to take Adam down. And if that means rounding up every single one of these people he's given abilities to and throwing them into a wormhole, then so be it."

Daniel smiled. "That's the spirit."

Cassie didn't look quite as impressed. "I don't know. It's..."

"We have to take difficult choices sometimes. We have to make the tough decisions. But right now, this is me taking responsibility. This is me and us stepping up and doing what's right for the planet. And I don't buy the crap about us not representing the people. We *are* people too. We just need to learn how to reconnect again."

More silence followed. I could hear an owl hooting somewhere nearby.

"So are you with me?" I asked.

Daniel looked at Cassie. Cassie looked back at him.

Then they both looked at me and nodded.

I felt a weight rise from my shoulders. The weight of questioning whether I was doing the right thing all along. "Good. I—"

I felt my phone ringing. That was weird. It was... it was the emergency phone. I only accepted calls from Ellicia, Damon, Avi and Dad on there.

I saw it was Ellicia.

"Ellicia?" I said. "What is it? Are you okay?"

"It's Damon," Ellicia said. "He—he's in big trouble. He needs your help."

[35]

A dam watched Kyle appear right outside Damon's place, just as he'd planned.

He could see the panic on Kyle's face. He could see just how worried he looked.

That made him smile. Because it meant that the plan must be coming together.

And there was nothing more wonderful than a plan coming together.

He looked over his shoulder at his followers standing behind him.

Then he turned back around and watched Kyle enter Damon's home.

He took a deep breath.

It was almost time to make his move.

Then, the world would be his.

When I got to Damon's, I knew right away that something was wrong.

I couldn't explain the feeling I had, other than it was an overwhelming sense of foreboding. Like I just knew something wasn't right. I'd had this feeling a hell of a lot in my life, but more so since I'd discovered my ULTRA abilities.

And when I'd had them since discovering my ULTRA abilities, they'd more often than not been totally right.

I stood outside his house and stared up through the windows. I couldn't see any movement, but after what Ellicia had said to me on the phone, there was something wrong with Damon. Apparently he'd called her and didn't sound too good, and that he needed my help immediately.

I wanted to press Ellicia for more information. I wanted to know more about Damon's predicament, and exactly what I was heading into.

But I didn't have time.

I walked up the steps and teleported my way through Damon's door.

His lounge was empty. The rest of the house seemed quiet,

too. I knew his parents were away, so that perhaps had something to do with it.

I looked around the lounge for a sign of him. Maybe he was hiding. Maybe he was hurt. God, I hoped not. I dreaded to think how I'd feel if he was hurt. I didn't want to let someone else I cared about down.

I left the lounge and headed into the kitchen.

I'd worried about this day ever since my first confrontation with Nycto. I feared that the time might come when someone I cared about got caught in the crossfire. And they had already, numerous times. Mom. Orion. My sister, Cassie, who'd remarkably turned out to be alive all along.

I didn't want to lose anyone else. Especially not my closest friend.

I searched the kitchen, but there was still no sign. I didn't want to shout in case someone was in here, watching. The house just *felt* empty, though. I had something of an intuition about me since developing my powers. Usually, my snap verdict was often right—as much as I didn't want to believe it a lot of the time.

But maybe this time, it was wrong.

Hopefully the whole thing was just a big misunderstanding. Then it dawned on me that Ellicia hadn't even told me Damon was at home at all. Maybe he was elsewhere. Maybe he'd been taken from his home, and someone was keeping him hostage.

I thought about teleporting over to Ellicia's when I heard footsteps upstairs.

I looked up at the ceiling.

There was a definite creaking around.

And then, just as quickly as I'd heard it, the creaking stopped.

On one hand, at least I knew someone was in.

On the other... it could be anyone.

I closed my eyes, took a deep breath, and activated my invisibility. Now was the time to take the stealthy route.

I crept up the stairs. Still I couldn't see anyone. The creaking was still going on though.

And it was coming from Damon's room.

My heart raced faster as I made my way to Damon's bedroom door. A whole host of scenarios circled my mind. I didn't know how I was going to find him in there. I didn't know what sort of condition I was going to find him in.

I just hoped to God he was okay.

I steadied my breathing, then I opened the bedroom door.

When I looked inside Damon's room, what I saw wasn't exactly what I expected.

Damon was standing at the other side of his bedroom.

He looked pale. Thinner and more gaunt than I remembered.

But more than anything, he looked like he'd been crying.

"Damon?"

I stepped closer to him and heard voices outside. I saw lights in the streets. I heard movement downstairs.

I looked back. "We need to—"

"I'm sorry, Kyle. I'm so sorry."

I looked back at Damon.

But this time, there was something different. Something very different.

Blood-red electricity sparked across his hands.

[37]

As much as I wanted to, I couldn't look my best friend in the eye. Not for long.

Because he had powers.

And by the looks of things, he was threatening to use them. Against me.

Outside, all around, I could hear footsteps approaching. It didn't take a genius to realize what those footsteps were. They were Adam's followers. They were on their way to surround me. All of this—the way I'd been brought here on the understanding that Damon needed help—was a setup.

Adam had got to Damon. The bastard had got to my best friend.

"Damon, don't—"

I saw Damon close his eyes, lift his hands, and fire in my direction.

I jumped out of the way of the electricity. It burned a hole in the back of Damon's room. I could smell burning; taste it, too.

"Please, Damon," I pleaded. "You don't have to—"

"I'm sorry."

He fired at me again. But once again, I jumped out of the

way of the electricity. Damon might've had powers, but he didn't have the same experience with them that I had. I knew I was stronger. I knew I could defeat him in a heartbeat, taking him down completely, if I wanted to.

But I didn't want to. Of course I didn't want to.

Damon was my best friend.

I dodged a few more of his attacks. As he fired at me, I heard the footsteps getting further up the stairs. I wanted to teleport away from here with Damon, but he wouldn't let me get close. He was reckless. If he wasn't careful, he was going to bring his whole house down.

"You need to stop this," I shouted. "We need to talk. Not fight."

"I've tried talking," Damon said. I saw then that he was full-on crying. Clearly this wasn't easy for him. "But you just don't hear me, man. You don't hear any of us. There's no other way anymore."

"There are other ways. Ways we can—"

Another blast of electricity flew at me.

I swung back.

This time, something was different.

I felt something smack into my chest. It hit me before I could do anything about it.

I fell to the floor, totally paralyzed, twitching and shaking. I struggled to breathe.

In the corner of my eye, I could see red electricity crackling all over my body. I knew right then that I'd been hit by Damon's powers.

My best friend's powers.

The taste of blood and sick filled my mouth. My head was banging, and I could barely hear a thing.

I tried to shift myself away from this place, but that biting electricity on my back just intensified.

I tried to create a wormhole, but it intensified even more.

Then I noticed there were lots of people in this room. Lots of people crowded into Damon's house. ULTRAs. ULTRAs that, not so long ago, weren't ULTRAs at all. They were people. People who felt betrayed and let down by the Resistance and me. People who had seen something in the words of Adam.

I was on my knees in front of my new leaders.

Damon was one of my new leaders.

My best friend.

I heard Damon's sluggish footsteps walking towards me. I didn't want to look up at him. I didn't want to face him after this.

But I knew I had to.

I looked into his tired eyes as he stood above me, hands sparking red electricity. His bottom lip shook. His cheeks were stained with tears.

"Please," I said. My voice was cracking now, too. "Damon, please. You're my best friend."

"That's why I'm doing this. Don't you see?"

I half-smiled and shook my head. "I get it. I get that—that you aren't happy. With the way things are. But Adam. He... he's using you, Damon. He's using you to get to me. And now he's got me. Unless you let me go. Please."

I saw a glimmer of our old lifelong bond and understanding in Damon's eyes. Just for a split second, I thought he was going to change his mind, and come around to my way of thinking.

Then he closed his eyes and sighed.

He lifted his hands.

"He'll be here soon. Don't... don't make me do anything."

Hearing Damon say those words was painful. Mortifying. I didn't know what to think or how to feel. I couldn't even feel betrayed.

Because I knew now that I'd done this. I'd formed this wedge between us.

I hadn't listened to what people like Damon wanted. I had been reckless. I'd caused chaos, with good intentions, sure. But chaos nonetheless.

Something had to change.

And to Damon and the rest of Adam's followers, Adam was that change.

"He'll take your powers away," I said. "The second he's done with you. He'll take your powers away."

Damon wiped his eyes. He tilted his head. "Then—then I guess that's fair."

"You know I'm not just going to back down right now. Don't you?"

Damon didn't budge.

"And you know what that means you're going to have to do. To your best friend."

Damon's cheeks flushed. He shook his head. "Don't. Please. Don't."

I closed my eyes.

I focused all of my energy on teleporting myself away from here, no matter how much it hurt with the paralyzing electricity singeing at my skin.

I gritted my teeth.

Bit the sides of my mouth.

"Kyle, don't—"

I heard a blast.

And as I crouched there, still trying to fight my way out of Damon's house, I was convinced that it was Damon who'd fired. I was convinced that he'd shot that electricity at me, and soon I'd be writhing around on the floor, totally broken, totally weak.

When I opened my eyes, I saw something entirely different.

38

Daniel Septer didn't like to admit it, but since he'd re-acquainted with his biological brother, he got a bad feeling whenever Kyle was in trouble.

He was in the middle of San Francisco when the latest sense of foreboding hit him square in the chest. He was watching the sun set at the side of the Orange County. It was a really nice, peaceful day. Of course, Daniel had to keep as low a profile as possible since Adam's followers were hunting down every ULTRA they could get their eyes on. The people wanted that, too. They wanted to see the current wave of ULTRAs all lose their powers in the hope that Adam could hand them over to them.

It made Daniel feel a little sick. He had to take his prover-bial hat off to Adam, of course. He'd really struck a nerve, and found a way to manipulate everyone into following him, for whatever end goal he had in mind.

But that was just the thing. There *was* an end goal for Adam. There was always an end goal where conquering the planet was concerned.

And dress it up however you like. Adam was conquering the

planet right now. It might be subtle, it might not be as bold and untidy an approach as Saint took.

But he was brainwashing the world to his way of thinking.

And the world was buying into it at an alarming rate.

Damned people. There was a reason Daniel thought about wiping the earth of them not so long back.

But hey. Everyone matured.

He listened to the silence of San Francisco, the sun shining down on him, and he got that feeling in the middle of his chest. It always brought on a funny taste in his mouth too. Like chlorine. He guessed it was something of a flashback to his earliest memory—being held underwater by his biological father, Orion, and Saint beside him.

It was a memory he'd only recently discovered. But when he'd discovered it, and discovered his real identity, his whole life had changed.

Cassie was his sister. And Kyle was his brother.

For better or for worse, Daniel was forced to put his long term plans for world domination on hold for that.

But hey. Long term plans were still long term plans.

He closed his eyes and teleported in the direction the feeling took him.

He was in New York in a flash. The contrast to San Francisco was depressing. It was dark in New York and raining.

He was somewhere he recognized, though.

Staten Island.

The street where Damon, Kyle's idiot best friend, lived.

Daniel tensed his fists when he elevated into the air and saw Damon and Kyle in Damon's room.

Damon was standing over Kyle. His hands were covered in... damn, was that electricity? So Damon was an ULTRA now? Daniel should've known the big guy would get too greedy.

He saw Damon lift his hands and point them right at Kyle's

face. And in that momentary flash, Daniel felt a sense of defensiveness over his older brother. Not to say they were best friends —they weren't. Their views on the world differed too much. They were just putting their differences aside for a few years of world peace. But neither of them was under any illusions about the truth.

One day, there would be war between them again.

It was just a matter of when.

But right now, it was important Kyle stayed alive.

Because Kyle was his brother. And Kyle was the ULTRAs' best hope against Adam.

It was a pity Daniel couldn't just leave humanity to destroy itself, and then realize the damage it'd done the hard way.

One day. One day.

Daniel flew in through Damon's window and slammed into the back of him.

He knocked him aside. Left him rolling in a mass of electrical sparks.

He jumped to his feet and felt time slowing down.

He punched the ULTRA behind Kyle in the face.

Then, when the rest of the surrounding ULTRAs lifted their hands and went to blast Daniel in their many ways, he bounced their powers right back at them.

Others, he soaked up the powers into one big ball, then sent it flying into that crowd.

Soon, there were only four left.

Daniel held out a hand to Kyle. "Come on. We have to get out of here."

Kyle looked totally distraught. Distraught like Daniel had never seen him. He took a bit of pleasure in his temporary defeat, but mostly he felt sympathy for his older brother. Clearly, Damon's betrayal had really hit him hard.

"Come on, man," Daniel said, hearing more footsteps emerge up the stairs. "We don't have much time."

Kyle stretched out his shaky hand and planted it in Daniel's.

He half-smiled at Daniel. And Daniel found himself half-smiling back at him.

"Thank you," Kyle said. He sounded weak. Bereft of confidence. "Thank..."

Daniel drifted out of the conversation then.

He drifted, because he saw something in the corner of his eyes.

Red.

He turned around and saw Damon firing electricity towards Kyle.

The electricity was too close to do anything about.

And judging by how weak Kyle was, he wouldn't survive any more of it.

Daniel did the only thing he could.

He did the only thing instinct forced him to do.

It wasn't the comfortable option.

Hell, it might not've even been the right option.

But it sure felt right.

He closed his eyes and threw himself in front of Kyle.

The red electricity hurtled at his chest.

For a moment, as Kyle struggled to drag him out of the way, Daniel thought maybe something had happened. Maybe the electricity had failed. Or maybe Kyle had found a way to repel it.

He opened his eyes and he saw the electricity make contact with his chest.

Then, he fell to his knees, and felt all his energy drift away.

39

I watched Damon's electricity fire into Daniel as he threw himself in front of me, and I knew right then from my emotions on the situation that everything had changed.

Daniel convoluted. His head flew back, knocked me right in the nose, which made me fall back and hit the floor in turn. He landed on top of me, his sparks of that paralyzing electricity singeing at me. I pulled myself away, even though I felt pretty weak myself. My head throbbed. I felt sick, especially now I could smell burning, and hear the groans coming from my brother.

"Come on," I said, pulling Daniel away. I wanted to teleport away from here, but I felt too exhausted, too weak. "You're strong. You can fight through the paralysis. If I can do it, you can."

At the opposite side of the room, Damon stood there and watched. He looked totally baffled about what to do next.

I pulled Daniel further to the other side of the room. The wall had broken away in the conflict, and I could feel the heat of flames surrounding me. "We have to go. We have to get out of here. Come on."

Daniel kept on shaking and struggling on the floor. I knew I had to do the heavy lifting myself.

"Don't go," Damon said.

I looked up at him. And right then, I felt nothing but hate. This guy wasn't my best friend anymore. He'd turned on me. He'd sold out to Adam. "You were supposed to trust me."

Damon shook his head. "How could I? When I saw what you were doing to the world?"

The pain of Damon's words made my stomach knot. I looked down at Daniel, who was unconscious. "Bye, Damon. You won't see me again."

He lifted his hands. "Wait—"

I teleported myself and Daniel away.

We landed a few blocks away. Dammit. I was trying to teleport us further, but clearly I was weak right now.

I felt the rain falling down on us as I dragged Daniel along. "Stay with me, brother. Stay with me."

I pulled him further, then teleported us away some more, aiming to reach the other side of the world.

We only made it about five hundred meters.

I looked over my shoulder. I could see someone following me then. Someone getting closer, in the shadows.

I turned around and teleported further away. Still, I was struggling to get outside of New York. Why was it? What was stopping me?

When I teleported even further, I realized why.

I was in the middle of a crowd of people. On a stage, in fact. There were masses of these people. All of them booing at me. Some of them hissing, and spitting. They were holding up placards:

BRING BACK MY SON!
MURDERER!
FALSE GODS!

As I stood there and listened to the angry roar of the crowd, I wasn't sure I'd ever felt as ashamed in my entire life.

"Come on," I said.

I went to pull Daniel away when I saw we weren't alone.

Adam was standing right beside us.

He lifted that gloved hand.

Out of instinct, I teleported above, so I was looking down on the events. Damn. I'd managed to teleport. Must've been pure instinct kicking in.

Only one problem.

Daniel was still down there on the stage.

I flew down towards Daniel when I saw Adam lift a hand.

"You come down here and you give up your powers. Right now."

I stopped, then. I stopped because as much as I wanted to save Daniel, I knew Adam wasn't going to let him go even if I did go down there. I knew he was too dangerous for Adam to allow to disappear.

I knew that if I flew down there, both of us were finished.

And I had a responsibility to the world to make sure I protected it from Adam.

Protected it from itself.

"No?" Adam said. "That's a shame. Then we'll get started."

I tried to shoot my way back down there, but I just bounced back off some kind of invisible force field that must've been set up. I punched at it. Tried to get through. But I couldn't. I just couldn't.

"Let him go!" I shouted.

Adam stood behind Daniel. He put his hands on his shoulders, and pressed him down onto the surrounded stage. "This is Daniel Septer. Nycto. You saw who he was flying with just then, didn't you? You saw who this terrorist is aligned with, didn't you? That's right. Glacies. Glacies the golden boy. The rumors are true."

I felt my stomach sink. I realized what was happening.

Adam was turning the people against me even more.

I rammed into that force field even more. I could feel it weakening. I had to be quick. I needed to get in there. I needed to get to Daniel.

I couldn't let Adam finish this speech.

"Nycto represents everything bad about the ULTRAs. He is responsible for so many deaths. And yet he flies *with* the gods who are supposed to police our world?"

"That's not true," I shouted.

Adam ignored me. As did everyone else. "He flies alongside the ULTRAs who claim they are looking out for us?"

Boos and jeers amongst the crowd.

Adam pushed Daniel down onto the stage. Daniel looked totally weak and broken. "Well I don't think that's right. I don't think it sends out the right message at all. Do you?"

A desperate cry of "no!"

So many people.

People I swore I'd protect.

None of them wanting my protection anymore.

"He flies with them and he destroys with them. Do we want any more of that?"

"No!"

Adam smiled as the crowd roared. I could tell he was enjoying this too much. And that unsettled me. Completely unsettled me.

He looked up at me, and that grin of his flickered. "We don't want any more of this. We don't want any more illegal rule. We don't want death. We want freedom. We want to be responsible for our own lives. We want to rule again."

A chorus of cheers, so loud and so deafening that the hair on my arms stood on end.

"So this is a symbol of the new way of doing things. This is a symbol of the new world order. This is a symbol of everything we once feared falling. Because I promise you, my people. We will never be afraid again."

From behind him, a woman walked up. She was short. Meek.

But she looked angry with Daniel.

Very angry.

"This is the new world order. And it starts right now."

The woman lifted her hands.

I saw a black liquid dripping down them.

"No!" I cried.

I tried to throw myself past that force field once more.

I tried to get in.

To get to Daniel.

The black liquid on the woman's hands got solid.

Then it glowed red.

"No!"

"This is the beginning," Adam said.

"Daniel!"

He looked up at me. Regained consciousness in that split second. And I felt relief because I knew he was quick enough to get away. I knew he was powerful enough to focus.

But then the woman fired those glowing red balls at him.

There was a flash of red light. It seared at my eyes, temporarily blinding me.

I heard a cheer from below, and it made my body collapse.

I knew what that cheer meant.

When my vision returned, beyond the cheering, celebratory crowds, and beyond Adam's raised arms and smiles, I saw a dark patch on the stage.

A patch where Daniel had once crouched.

Daniel Septer was gone.

Nycto was gone.

My brother was gone.

40

Machu Picchu would look a hell of a lot more amazing if I didn't have a dark cloud hanging over me.

A dark cloud of memories of what had happened.

I sat right at the top of the Andes. It was hard to breathe up here, what with the difference in altitude. Of course, I was used to sudden changes in altitude. A part of my powers was that I could change my body's receptiveness to altitude, and easily adapt to new climates with a click of my fingers.

But I didn't change anything right now.

I just sat at the top of the hills opposite Machu Picchu and let the sickness fill my body.

The silence was comforting. I didn't want any more outside noise. Not anymore. I was dealing with enough as it was already.

All I wanted to do was lay low and stay far, far away from trouble.

A part of me wanted to go back to Staten Island. Whenever I was in a tough moment, I always clung to the hope that no matter how bad it got, I could just go back home.

But home had changed. Home had changed a lot.

I'd watched Damon develop powers.

And I'd watched him use those powers against me.

It made me cold just to think of it. Just a year ago, the pair of us had been at school. Naturally, I'd scrapped school since I'd taken on a very different kind of education. But it seemed like so much had changed in such a short space of time.

I wanted to go back. I wanted things to be the way they used to be. Simpler. Less responsibility.

Now, I knew things would never be the same ever again.

I stood up and walked away from the edge of the mountain edge. I walked for miles and miles, rubbing the soles of my feet right down. I could've healed them. But again, I didn't want to right now. I didn't want to use my powers for anything. Powers had got me into this mess in the first place.

I just wanted to be Kyle Peters again.

But then a foreboding sense hit me when I thought of that, too. Because I could *never* be my old self again, not just because my circumstances had changed, but because of who I was. My identity was known to the world—my *real* identity. I was a celebrity, whether I liked it or not. Just not the kind of celebrity I wanted to be.

And anyway, I'd slipped way, way out of the public's good graces. I was like... actually, no. I won't say their name. Libel's a crapper, right?

I walked a little further when I saw a group of ULTRAs in the distance.

They were swooping down over the ancient Peruvian sites and knocking them to pieces. I could hear them laughing, whooping and cheering. Clearly they hadn't had their abilities for long, but they weren't wasting much time in using their abilities for bad rather than good.

I tensed my fists and felt ice singe at the tips of my fingers. A freezing sensation stretched up my forearms. They were causing chaos. I needed to go over there and stop that chaos.

Then I saw what'd probably happen. I'd get into a fight with them. Someone would get badly hurt. Then I'd get blamed not only for hurting someone else, but for destroying an ancient site.

I sighed, and unclenched my fists.

I'd had enough of using my powers to help other people out, especially with the way they were repaying the good faith.

I watched the ULTRAs destroy that place that was so many years etched in history.

I took a deep breath, and turned around.

I was through with Glacies.

Damon was gone. Alive, but gone.

Daniel Septer, Nycto, my biological brother, was gone. Really gone.

And Kyle Peters, the life I'd lived, was gone. In all its forms.

I walked off into the hills.

I wasn't fighting anymore.

41

Adam stood over Hong Kong at the top of the International Commerce Centre and stared down at his army of newly transformed ULTRAs.

He looked at the vast expanse of them from left to right. There were so many of them. An army of thousands. And the ones right here were his most loyal, the most committed to the cause.

Originally, he'd just wanted to convert as many people to his way of thinking. After all, he had a cause. Something people believed in. The Resistance were unelected gods. And sure, they'd done *some* good for the world. But they'd exceeded their stay on this planet.

He wanted to give a voice back to the people. He wanted them to see what was happening right before their eyes.

Now they'd seen that, he wanted something more.

He looked beyond the vast array of ULTRAs right in front of him. Beyond, he could see the clouds thickening. He thought about the many ULTRAs still out there. The original ULTRAs that'd been a part of the Resistance. But also the ULTRAs who were newly formed, too. The ones he'd given powers to, but who hadn't shown any evidence that they were fit to take responsibility for their powers.

Now, Adam couldn't help but worry about them. He'd given them a key to destruction. He wanted to take that power back. He wanted to be in control again.

He had an idea how he wanted to do it. And in the end, he'd always had his eye on the prize. Kyle Peters, or Glacies, as he was known. He'd been close to him many times. But now, he knew he needed to ramp up his assault.

Not just because he wanted his powers.

But because he wanted to bury him.

Forever.

He thought back to Daniel Septer. The confrontation and stand-off he'd had with him. As he'd watched Alison charge up her powers and prepare to eliminate him forever, he'd seen an opportunity to step in and take his powers away, becoming almost as powerful as Kyle.

There'd been a moment of crisis. A moment, where Adam saw what was in front of him and faced a real dilemma. Take Daniel's powers away, and be *almost* as strong as Kyle?

Or wait for Kyle to take his powers away, and be the strongest of all?

Then, out of nowhere, there'd been an explosion. Adam felt it radiating from his palms.

When the flash of light cleared from Adam's view, Daniel was nothing more than a mark on the ground.

Alison had finished the job that Adam had made her start.

The chance of taking Daniel's powers was gone.

It wasn't an ideal end for Adam. After all, he'd had an opportunity to become much more powerful.

But Daniel wasn't the endgame. Nobody but Kyle was the endgame.

And he wasn't giving up on that endgame now that Kyle was weak and on the run.

Nearly as strong as Kyle?

That wasn't what Adam wanted.

He wanted to *be* as strong as Kyle.

And he was going to achieve that goal, very soon.

"There are ULTRAs out there hellbent on our destruction," Adam shouted.

His voice boomed from the top of the International Commerce Centre, down onto the streets filled with his followers, all recently converted, all worshiping him.

"We can't allow them to fight much longer. Because they don't fight in the interests of the people. They don't fight in *our* interests."

A cheer. A roar from the crowd.

It made the hairs on Adam's arms stand on end.

"As long as those enemies are out there, we face the risk of losing. I have full confidence in us. Believe me. But all of us know we're not totally safe and clear until we defeat one ULTRA. Kyle Peters. Glacies."

A bigger roar. A roar that was total music to Adam's ears.

They believed in him. They were on his side.

They worshiped him.

So why was he so afraid?

Why was he so paranoid?

He swallowed a lump in his throat as the first specks of rain started to fall. "What we have to do won't be pretty. There'll be some loss. There'll be some chaos. Hell, there'll be some destruction. But the way I see it, a little more chaos is worth it in return for us getting our world back."

"Yeah!" some of the crowd cheered. Hands started lighting up, a whole cocktail of powers and abilities sparking right before Adam's eyes.

A cocktail he'd started.

"I say it's worth all those risks if it means saving humanity. Don't you?"

More cheers. More applause.

Adam smiled. He smiled, as the voices got louder. He smiled as ice and fire and water and electricity shot up into the sky. This was the uprising he'd created. And finally it was taking shape.

Finally, it was happening.

Adam felt a smile spread across his face. But it was a smile filled with anger. With frustration. Because he didn't have what these people—these ULTRAs—had. He didn't have any abilities. Just a piece of government technology on his arm that gave him the power to take other abilities away.

A piece of technology that would be worthless when he absorbed someone else's powers for himself.

He knew exactly whose powers he wanted.

He knew exactly where his conquest to share abilities with the world—to democratize powers—ended.

"It's time to take our planet back," Adam shouted.

"Yeah!"

"It's time to fight back against our oppressors."

"Yes!"

"It's time to destroy every single ULTRA in our path."

42

Ellicia saw the news about the attacks across America and she knew she wasn't safe.

The afternoon sun peeked in through her blinds, which were closed. Her room was warm and stuffy. She wanted nothing more than to get outside in the fresh air. She wanted to spend time with Kyle, just how she used to.

But she knew things had changed with Kyle. Kyle couldn't be the person she wanted him to be. He couldn't even be the person *he* wanted to be.

He had responsibilities, now. Duties.

The Kyle Peters Ellicia fell in love with was long gone.

In his place, someone she couldn't help being frightened of.

Not because she thought he'd hurt her. She knew Kyle. He'd never hurt her. But she was frightened of him because she worried just how far he'd go to win his side of the fight.

And if the rumors that Daniel Septer—Nycto—was gone were true, then she didn't know what to think at all.

She just hoped Kyle hadn't taken it too badly. After all, he hadn't long been aligned with Daniel himself.

She walked across her bedroom back at her parents' place

and looked into her suitcase. She'd stuffed tons of clothes inside it. She wasn't sure where exactly she was going to go, but she knew she had to get away from here.

She looked back at the television. The sound of the voices in the studio all bouncing off one another made her head hurt, filled her mouth with the taste of sick. She saw the reports of the attacks—random attacks in random parts of the country—and she knew it couldn't be good news. It made the hairs on her arms stand on end because it reminded her of another dark time.

The night the ULTRAs and the ULTRAbots went to war.

And she knew damn well how that ended.

She tried to close her suitcase, but it was too stuffed to force shut. She sighed, opened it up again, and threw a few clothes onto her bedroom floor. She kept on going, furious, caught in a daze. She felt tears building up. How had it come to this? How had everything reached this point?

When she got to the middle of the suitcase, she saw a photograph.

She picked it out of the case and held it close to her face.

It was a photograph of her and Kyle in Central Park. She remembered it as one of the first dates they'd been on, right by the lake. Kyle was squinting, and his ice cream was melting down his hand. Ellicia was giggling, and both her eyes were closed, too.

But as she looked at that photograph, which she loved so much she'd had it printed, she smiled. That was them, in a nutshell. That was Goofy Kyle, in a nutshell.

All that was gone.

No. All that couldn't be gone.

They had something special. There had to be something left. There had to—

A knock at her front door.

She turned around and faced her bedroom door. It was

wide open.

She felt goose pimples on her skin. She swore she'd closed her bedroom door. And there was no chance anyone else had opened it. Her parents were away for the night, so she was house sitting. She had an apartment of her own now, which Kyle had kindly sorted out for her. Anywhere in the world, he'd told her. Anywhere. And she just couldn't bring herself to turn her back on Staten Island. She just couldn't run away in fear from New York.

But now, her thoughts were focused on one thing.

Who had opened that door?

She sat there in that weird silence that always followed a loud, shocking noise. She listened for footsteps outside her house. She listened for a cough or some kind of chatter. She just needed to know if there was someone out there, still, and if so, who it was.

Heart pounding, Ellicia took a few calming breaths. She didn't have to go down there. It was probably just the mailman delivering a parcel. She could go collect the parcel later. She just didn't want to answer the door. She didn't want to—

Another knock.

This time, louder. Harder.

Ellicia stepped off her bed and walked out of her bedroom. She crept across the hallway, keeping as quiet as she could. She wanted to get to the peephole and take a look through.

But already, as she descended her stairs, she got the feeling that there was someone else inside, and she got that awful sensation telling her to get out of there. Fast.

She reached the bottom of the stairs. Her heart raced even faster now. She didn't want to go over to that door, but she could see a vague silhouette behind it.

She had to know who it was.

She had to see.

She closed her eyes. Gritted her teeth.

Then she moved her eye toward the peephole.

When she saw who it was, she felt her shoulders sink, and the tightness of her body release.

She opened the door. "Avi. Jesus, you scared me."

Avi looked terrified. He was pale and shaking. He kept on looking over his shoulder.

"Avi? What is it?"

"There's someone following me. I swear."

Ellicia popped her head out of the front door. "I can't see—"

"I just know. I just know."

When Ellicia made eye contact with him, she had to admit that she knew exactly what Avi meant.

She just knew someone was watching, too. She knew someone was coming.

"We have to get out of this city," she said, turning around and going back into the house. "If the stories of Adam's followers attacking the ULTRAs are true, then he'll want Kyle and maybe even Damon dead, too."

"Screw those guys," Avi said. "They ain't nothin' anymore."

Ellicia shook her head. "That's not true. They're your best friends. And I'm not gonna let you give up on them."

She started to climb the stairs. She waited for Avi's footsteps to follow, but she didn't hear any.

"Come on," she said. "Give me a lift with my stuff. Avi?"

She turned around.

Avi wasn't standing there anymore.

In his place, a tall, slim guy with dark, curly hair and luscious green eyes.

He had his hands behind his back. His smile was infectious but icy. Like there was nothing behind it.

"Hello, Ellicia," he said. "I'm Adam. It's a pleasure to finally meet you."

43

I sipped back my eighth beer and felt so much better about myself.

If only that were true.

Yes, I was sipping on a drink. I was in some rundown South American bar, which other than me, was completely empty. But instead of beer, it was Coca Cola I was drinking.

When I'd got here, I saw how empty the place was and expected the bartender to just hand over the booze. After all, I had my hood up. I was pretty well built these days. He had to believe I was legally able to drink—or at least he had to be short enough on business that he'd just hand over a pint, right?

But he hadn't. He'd looked into my eyes and told me I couldn't drink if I had no ID. Of course I didn't have any ID. Usually, my face was ID these days, and I wasn't too keen to go revealing that so much right now. And sure, I could head somewhere else, or just find a way to manipulate the guy into believing I was legally able to drink, or, hell, I could just beat the guy until he poured me a beer.

But I wasn't in the mood for fighting. I wasn't in the mood for using any of my powers. Not now. Not ever again.

All I wanted was to jump from place to place around the world and keep as low a profile as possible.

After all, when I did anything else, I was dangerous.

I sipped back the slimy Coke. It tasted off, if it was possible for Coke to take off. It was like it'd been stuck in the back of this place for years. It wasn't particularly cold, either, which confirmed my fears that it hadn't been in a fridge.

But I didn't care. Course I didn't care.

I listened to the tropical music playing. All around the bar, mosquitos and flies flew about. Some of them head butted my sweaty body, so I just wafted them away. Above my head, a rotating fan did a terrible job of cooling the air.

The bartender kept on glaring over at me.

When we made eye contact, he tended to look away.

But this time, he stayed focused.

"I know who you are," he said.

I tensed my fists and got ready for trouble.

He cleaned the inside of a glass with a towel. "Hey. Don't you go trashing my bar. You are free to drink here. I'm just saying. I know who you are."

He sounded calm when he spoke. And that made me wonder if actually he wasn't so bad after all. That maybe he was indeed cool with me being here.

"So you're a villain after all, hmm?"

"I guess if the media say that's what I am, then that's what I am." I went to drink some more of the warm, syrup-like Coke.

"You know, the media did the same to us."

"Hmm?"

"Colombia. The media make us look bad. They say we nothing but drug barons. They say there's no order here. But that's not true. We have problems, but so does everywhere. And we are getting stronger. We are getting better."

I forced a smile, eager to get out of this place and away from this man's harassment. "Well good for you."

"We didn't just flick a switch and things were okay, though. We earned it. We had to work hard, all of us, the whole country. And yes. We still have problems. But we're better now. Because we knew that if we wanted respect, we had to earn it."

The bartender walked away from me towards the back of the bar. He emerged with a half-pint glass, and poured it half full with beer. He pushed it across the bar, right in front of me.

I frowned. "What's this?"

"Half of a half pint. Don't want you drinking and flying. Not in my country."

I sighed, tilted my head, and lifted the glass. "Thanks. I guess."

He nodded, that constant stern look still etched across his face. Then he disappeared from the bar.

I went to drink the beer. The closer it got to my lips, the more uncertain I got about it. Was this who I wanted to be? Kyle Peters, former superhero, present occupation: drunk bum. Glacies, the alcoholic ULTRA. Was that the legacy I really wanted to pass down to those I wanted to inspire?

I thought about Cassie, Vortex, Stone, and Ember, wherever they were. I knew if they saw me like this, they'd be ashamed. Because no matter what, we were supposed to fight for what we believed in. Even if what we believed in meant handing ourselves over to the government.

My duty was to the people of Earth, though. And they'd spoken loudly. So loudly that my best friend had tried to take my powers away and destroyed my biological brother in the process.

But then that was no peaceful world. That wasn't the idealistic vision of the future the protesting people wanted or deserved.

That was just the power-crazed fantasy of a megalomaniac.

Another false god telling the people how to serve him.

I put the beer down when the grainy CRT television from like, the nineteen thirties, caught my eye.

There was breaking news in New York. Attacks on ULTRAs. Only they weren't random attacks. They were co-ordinated. By Adam.

I saw the next shot cut away from the footage near Central Park.

I recognized this place.

It was right outside my dad's old mechanics. Right on Staten Island.

Adam's followers were in the streets.

I felt dread cover me. I wanted to stay put. I didn't want to cause any more death, any more destruction.

But then if Adam's followers were in Staten Island and the rumors were that they were hunting down the original ULTRAs, then that meant they could question those closest to me.

That meant Avi, Ellicia, and Dad were in danger.

And it meant Cassie was in danger.

And maybe even Damon was in danger.

I remembered what the bartender had said. *"We didn't just flick a switch and things were okay, though. We earned it. We had to work hard, all of us, the whole country. And yes. We still have problems. But we're better now. Because we knew that if we wanted respect, we had to earn it."*

And he was right. He was totally right.

I might have a negative image.

People might hate me.

But I wasn't winning the haters back by sitting around here and getting drunk.

I went to teleport away from Colombia when the door to the bar opened.

The second the massive crowd walked in, I knew from the looks on their faces that they were ULTRAs.

Adam's followers.

"Sorry, Glacies."

I turned around.

The bartender stood behind the bar.

His hands were covered in throwing knives.

And he was getting ready to throw them.

44

D amon zipped his hoodie right up over his chin and pulled his hood over his eyes. He didn't want anyone to see him. Not since he'd heard the news.

It was the middle of the afternoon, but the early sun was making way for thick, gray clouds. It made it feel like night in New Jersey. He'd been staying in New Jersey to keep a low profile. But now rumors were going around that Adam's followers were hunting down the first wave of ULTRAs—Kyle's lot—in full force.

And as safe as Damon felt for not being a part of that first wave, he still didn't want to be a part of what Adam was doing.

Because now, he couldn't shake the guilt he felt for everything he'd done, and for how everything had unfolded.

Rain lashed down on him as he walked through Wharton State Forest. He could smell that mixture of humid air and dampness, which was supposed to be a nice, relaxing scent, but he was far from relaxed right now. He felt weak. He hadn't eaten in days.

All because of those changes that'd occurred inside his body.

All because of the powers Adam had given him.

He'd always thought it'd be pretty cool to have abilities. Especially since his best friend was the strongest damned ULTRA in the world. Hard not to feel a little jealous there.

But now he had powers, he saw the responsibility that came with them, as well as the potential for accidental destruction.

For the first time in a long time, he actually felt something like pity and sympathy for Kyle. Because as much destruction as he'd caused, as much recklessness he'd been a part of, Damon saw now that Kyle probably had only been acting in the best interests of the world. The destruction that came with it, unfortunate as it was, was just a side effect of powerful weapons like him.

And Kyle really was still just a kid like him.

He kept on walking further into the forest. He figured he'd just hide away in here as long as he could. Again, he was pretty sure he was safe. He wasn't a First Wave, as they were now calling the ULTRAs who emerged around the same time as Kyle. He wasn't ever a member of the Resistance, either. He'd just been Kyle's friend—Kyle's best friend.

But he'd torn all that apart.

Shit. *He'd* torn all that apart.

He stopped. Put his hands on his legs, gasping for air as the rain fell down even heavier on him.

He'd betrayed Kyle. Kyle had trusted him all this time and he'd stabbed him in the back. He saw it for what it was, now. Sure, he'd just been looking out for other people. Sure, he told himself it was just the right thing for Kyle because it'd mean he wouldn't get himself in any more trouble.

But it was still what it was. Betrayal. A stab in the back.

A stab that ended their amazing friendship, surely forever.

He tried to steady his breathing, but he was well in the grips of a panic attack. His heart thumped so heavily he thought it might burst out of his chest like that little creature in the first Alien movie. Every breath he took was forced and labored. He felt dizzy and sick. He just wanted to be away from all this. He just wanted to put it behind him.

But then he thought about Kyle. He thought about him out there, hunted by the world. He might not totally agree with Kyle's methods, but Kyle was still a damn good guy. He was his best friend. Damon had the abilities to fight with him. Sure, he was pretty clumsy, but Kyle needed all the help he could get.

So he'd go to him. He'd find him, wherever he was. Or he'd find a way of reaching out to him. Damn, he'd do something.

He had to get to Kyle.

He had to apologize.

And he had to fight with him.

When he stood up, breathing back to normal and much more composed, he saw someone opposite him.

There were five people.

Four of them were on their knees.

One of them was standing.

The guy standing was familiar. He'd recognize those green eyes from a mile away. He felt his guts turn, and goose pimples spread across his arms. When he tried to step away, he noticed movement to his left, to his right, behind him, and he knew he was surrounded.

It wasn't just Adam that terrified Damon.

It was the people crouching in front of him.

"Hello again," Adam said. He walked in front of the three people crouched there. "Not gonna say hello to your friends? How rude."

Damon looked at Ellicia's terrified eyes.

He looked at the tears on Avi's cheeks.

He looked at the defeat on Cassie's face.

And he looked at the purple bruises on Kyle's dad's skin.

"No?" Adam said. He sighed. "Oh well. Good. We can get to the real reason I'm here."

Damon tried to walk away, but someone grabbed him. He couldn't move or use his powers.

Adam stepped over him. "I think you've served your purpose. And you served it really well."

He put his hand on Damon's head.

"But now it's time for a new purpose. Let's get started."

45

"Just give it up, Kyle. It's over. You've lost."

I stood in the middle of the Colombian bar. The bartender who'd served me not long ago, given me life advice not long ago, now had a handful of knives —knives that he'd sprouted from his own palms. He was pointing them at me.

And all around me, a crowd of ULTRAs. Adam's followers.

I looked around at the crowd, one by one. Some of them had electricity coming from their hands. Others had fire. Some had ice. Some of them didn't have anything visible, which meant that they were the ones to really watch out for.

But they all looked tough. And they all looked angry.

And collectively, they might just be too much for me to fight through.

"So there's two ways we play this," the bartender said. "Either you surrender, and we take you back to Adam. Or you fight, and we... well. We take you back to Adam. Only much more broken and bruised."

"Surely not a great idea working behind a bar with knives for hands?"

Knifey sniggered. For the first time, that totally serious expression had completely dropped. "You are a terrible joker, Kyle. But now we are going to have a lot of fun with you. A lot of laughs."

Quicker than I could speak, Knifey fired a blast of knives at me.

I ducked. Then I stopped them in midair, snapping them with my telekinesis, making them fall to the floor around me.

I heard footsteps coming toward me. In the corner of my eye, someone with hammers for feet. Massive hammers.

She pulled back of those hammers and went to kick me.

I grabbed the hammer. I took its full weight, absorbing it, the shockwaves kicking through my body.

Then I twisted her leg around and threw her, hammer-first, back into the crowd of ULTRAs.

I felt something in my stomach, then. Not quite a stabbing, but the sense that something—or someone—was close.

I jumped aside.

Just in time.

Someone had been invisible right beneath me.

And then had a sharp iron rod in their hands.

I jolted to my feet. The crowd of ULTRAs was all firing at me now and running at me. I focused individually on each bolt of energy, water, electricity, fire, all coming toward me, and I soaked them up into mini-wormholes. I felt that wormhole getting bigger. I felt the charge getting stronger. I felt it get so strong that it was ready to release, ready to let go, ready to blow this place—

A sharp, hot pain stuck into my back.

I gasped. My grip on that wormhole dropped, and the power I'd been charging to defeat these remaining ULTRAs disappeared out of my reach.

I fell to my knees. I could taste blood.

When I looked at the front of my body, I saw something poking out of it, right at the diaphragm.

It was a knife.

I tried to steady my breathing and heal myself, gasping for air.

But then I felt ice smack me in the face.

Then I felt fists punching at me, hard.

And before I knew it, I was on my back, a mountain of Adam's followers all crawling above me, like termites.

I felt the knife pushing further into me. I knew I needed to heal myself. But the more I focused on healing that, the more my guard dropped and the more open I was to being hurt in other ways.

I closed my eyes and thought about Ellicia. I thought about Dad. I thought about everyone I cared about back home, and what Adam might do to them if he found them.

I thought about Cassie.

I'd worked so hard to get her back.

I couldn't risk losing her again.

I focused on that pain in my chest and I let out a cry.

When I cried, I felt energy surging out of my body faster than I'd ever felt. I heard swooshing noises, and the ground started to shake. The roof of the bar lifted away. The whole place was falling down.

And then I saw why.

As I continued screaming, I saw a wormhole right above the bar. A jet black wormhole bigger than any I'd created.

It was sucking everyone up into it.

I pushed even further, as agonizing as the wound in my chest was. I kept going as the ULTRAs struggled to hold on, until eventually there were only four left.

One of them was the bartender. Knifey.

He gripped onto the bar with his knife hands and for the first time since I'd met him, he actually looked worried.

"Thank you," I mumbled.

He frowned. "For what?"

"For making me realize."

Then the bar snapped away and Knifey disappeared into the wormhole along with the rest of his cronies.

I watched them fly into it, out of sight.

Then I closed the wormhole.

The ground went still. In the place of cracking and splitting, silence.

But my breathing was still tough. Still totally ropey.

I sat up. Put my hands on the back of the knife. I held my breath and went to squeeze my eyes shut.

Before I did, I saw the news on that grainy television that'd somehow stayed standing, unlike the majority of the rest of the bar.

On the television, I saw Adam.

In front of him, Avi. Damon. Ellicia. Dad.

And Cassie.

"You have one hour, Kyle," Adam said. There was a crowd of people around him, all cheering. "One hour to turn yourself in. To hand yourself over. For the greater good."

More cheering. Adam looked around, soaking up the applause.

Then he looked right back into the camera.

"If you don't show in the next hour, if you don't turn yourself over, then you know what happens."

He walked over to the back of Avi and put a hand on his head.

"They die."

The crowd roared.

The footage went totally grainy.

Then, it cut to static.

I stood there in the middle of the fallen Colombian bar.

The knife wasn't in my back anymore.

My breathing was fine.

Without even thinking, I'd totally healed myself.

Everyone I loved was in danger.

Everyone I loved was going to die.

I couldn't let that happen.

46

I looked down at Krakatoa and couldn't believe how much had happened in the last year.

The remains of Krakatoa were pretty amazing to look at. I mean, this used to be a volcano. It used to be the site of one of the most devastating eruptions in human history. It was true evidence of the power nature had over man.

Now?

It was nothing more than a mass of broken rock and debris.

Rock and debris that, a year ago, I'd buried Nycto under.

At least I thought I'd buried him under.

I listened to the sea crashing against the rocks that used to make up Krakatoa. I could taste the saltwater on my lips, which were dry and cracked as it was. I was shaky, and I felt battered and bruised. More than anything, I just wanted to be over in New York, helping fight for Dad, Ellicia, Damon, Avi, and Cassie. I knew I'd been told I had an hour to save them, and twenty minutes had already passed.

But there was something else I needed to do.

I lifted my hands. My arms were still stiff from the fight I'd had in Colombia not long ago. I bit down on my chapped lip

204 / MATT BLAKE

and focused on those rocks below. Slowly, I started to pull them apart.

If you think telekinesis is easy, you're wrong. The objects you're moving are still tough as hell, it's just you have a slight advantage of not having to actually grab them with your physical hands.

Luckily, I was strong as it was. That was just part of being Glacies.

But still, it wasn't easy.

I felt my chest splitting as I pulled the rocks apart and I knew I had to be careful. I'd been stabbed right through my chest not long ago. Although I'd healed myself, I didn't want to risk agitating the wound any more.

But I had to pull these rocks apart.

I felt rain splash against me and a bitter taste filled my mouth. I felt bad about what I was doing, and about what I was going to do. I knew it was risky and dangerous. But I knew for a fact that I needed help from forces way more powerful than me.

I pulled the rocks right apart. Then, I looked up into space.

I remembered what Damon asked me a week ago. A week that seemed so long ago, to think about it. I remembered when he asked if I'd ever teleported into space. It made my chest tingle and my legs shake, just thinking about it. I knew how much of a risk it was.

But I knew what I needed to do now.

Or at least, what I needed to try and do.

I held my breath.

Then, I shifted all my energy into creating a massive wormhole in the middle of Krakatoa beneath me.

I watched the sea start to swirl, like a whirlpool was forming.

I watched electricity sparkle at the surface of the water.

I watched a vast void opening.

I steadied my focus, held my breath some more as I opened up that void.

I knew what was through there.

I knew what I needed to do when I got through there.

I thought of Dad. Ellicia. Everyone I loved.

I was doing this for them.

But not just them.

I was doing this for the world, whether the world realized it or not.

I closed my eyes. Wiped away a tear.

Then I let go of my focus and allowed the wormhole to suck me into its suffocating clutches.

[47]

A dam looked at his watch and saw there were only ten
minutes remaining.
He couldn't help but crack a smile.
He looked across the vast expanse of Staten Island. Everywhere he looked, in the glow of the sun, which burned through
the rainclouds, he saw people. All of them were holding up
banners with his face on. All of them were cheering his name.

He'd never felt so powerful or so mighty in his life.

But there was still something missing. And that something
was Kyle Peters. Glacies.

He looked ahead, at the tall building he stood on. In front of
him, the people he knew Kyle cared about most. His dad. His
girlfriend. His sister. His two best friends.

So where was he?

Why wasn't he here?

He walked over to Damon, who he'd placed beside Ellicia.
He could see the red electricity sizzling at the energy-
suppressing ties around Damon's wrists, the same kind he'd put
around Cassie's wrists. He knew they weren't breaking through
those ties anytime soon. They weren't strong enough.

"How does it feel knowing he isn't coming for you?" Adam whispered.

Nobody responded.

He leaned closer to the side of Ellicia. "How does it feel knowing your hero has given up on you?"

"He hasn't given up on us."

Adam turned around.

It was Damon who'd spoken.

"What did you say?"

"I said he hasn't given up on us," Damon said. He stared straight ahead, over the side of the building, into the crowd. "He'd never give up on us. No matter what."

Adam felt his grin stretching further. He reached over and put a hand on Damon's shoulder. He could feel Damon's powers just beneath his glove. He wanted to drag them away, but at the same time, he wanted to be strong for when Kyle arrived, so he could finally take those powers that were rightly his. "Well. There's... eight minutes left now. And no sign of your hero. So he'd better get a move on."

Adam walked away from his hostages. He stood at the edge of the building and looked down at the armies of liberated people. He felt so proud when he saw his followers. So many people he'd gifted. Even the ones who hadn't been converted to ULTRAs believed in what he was doing.

He was democratizing powers.

He was giving the people something to believe in.

"Soon, we will be free," Adam called. "All of us will be free from fear. Glacies will be with us no more. And we can share what he has. All of us."

A cheer from the crowd. The cheers always made the hairs on the back of Adam's neck stand on end. Of course, he was lying about his plans to share Kyle Peters' powers with others.

He'd done enough sharing with other people. He deserved a little something to himself.

And he'd get it.

"He'll come for you."

Adam turned around.

This time, it was Kyle's father who spoke.

He looked up at Adam through bruised, tired eyes. He didn't look scared. Just ground down by the world. Like he'd been through so much crap that he just didn't care what happened to him anymore.

"Got something to say for yourself?" Adam asked.

"I said, he'll come for you."

"I heard—"

"And when he comes for you, he'll take you down. Because he cares about people way more than you ever have. And he's much, much more of a hero than you'll ever be."

Adam smiled. For a moment, he could feel Kyle's father getting under his skin.

Then the roar of the crowd invaded his soul all over again, and everything felt okay.

"We'll see." He looked down at his watch. "Four minutes. Four minutes until you—"

Then he heard the massive explosion above.

He looked up at the sky.

He saw the mass of purple right in the middle of the clouds.

He saw the spiraling hole burned into the middle of the atmosphere.

He saw the wormhole, and he saw the speck in the middle of it.

He knew what that speck was.

Who that speck was.

"Well now," Adam said. "Look who's late to the party."

[48]

I shot down to the rooftop of the Staten Island building and stood opposite Avi, Damon, Dad, Cassie, and Ellicia.

And Adam.

The rain lashed down heavily. Behind me, on the ground, I could hear boos and shrieks the second I appeared. Some of the crowd had powers, so were floating at the side of the building. I heard the crowd getting more angsty. They clearly worshiped Adam after all his brainwashing. And in a way, I couldn't blame them. He'd given them so much power.

Or at least, the illusion of power.

In their eyes, all I'd done was shown them the way. I was the past. Adam was the future.

It was my job to make sure they didn't believe that for long.

I took a deep breath of the humid air and looked Adam in the eye. "My people. Let them go."

Adam smiled. He was soaked with rain, but his curly locks looked totally unaffected. "Your *people*? That's funny. You see, I swear you have some other people somewhere too. Your Resistance. Right?"

I tried not to think about the Resistance. I didn't know

where they were. If they were in hiding, I couldn't blame them. I hoped wherever they were, they were okay.

But this was my challenge. This was my fight.

Adam was mine to defeat.

"And what about the people on the ground?" Adam said. "The people hovering at the side of the building? The people you're supposed to represent? What do they think?"

Their cheers for Adam caught my attention all over again. I had to admit it was unnerving how much they'd been won over to his side and his cause. It sure made my fight a lot harder. "They don't know what they want. Or what you really are."

"Oh," Adam said, a feigned look of shock across his face. "They don't know what they want? You really think so ill of their intelligence, do you?"

"I didn't—"

"Hear those boos? They are boos against you. That is the sound of the very people you claim you fight for telling you they don't want you anymore. You don't make choices for them anymore. You don't speak for them anymore."

The boos were so loud that my head hurt. I looked across at the people kneeling in front of Adam. I looked into Damon's shamed eyes, so pitiful, so sorry. I looked at Avi's fear. I saw Dad's pride in me, right to the bitter end. I saw Cassie looking at me just as she had nine years ago, like she was scared not just for herself, but for me.

And then I saw Ellicia.

Ellicia was the only one of these people looking at me with a smile on her face. I saw the light in her eyes. The same light I'd see when Damon and I went to that soccer game a year ago. A year in which so much had happened. A year in which so much had changed.

She looked at me with faith.

"I understand I don't speak for people. Not anymore. I get that."

Some of the boos receded. An air of confusion radiated, like nobody expected me to say what I'd said. I could hear what they were asking. Was I giving up? Was I handing myself over?

Even Adam looked a little confused. He tried to keep that smile, but I could see it twitching, faltering at the edges. "That's admirable."

"I don't speak for the people. And I understand people should be able to choose. They should have a decision in who leads them."

The boos started to turn to cheers. But I could tell they were cheers at my impending resignation, if that's what they were suspecting.

"And I apologize," I said, my throat clamming up as the breeze grew stronger. I looked right into Ellicia's eyes. "I apologize for the bad decisions I've made."

I turned to Damon. My eyes were clouded with tears now.

"I apologize for the chaos I've caused. For the destruction I've caused. For the people I've let down."

The cheers were in full assault now.

Adam looked well and truly thrown. Like he was expecting a fight.

I walked towards him. Stood right opposite him. I looked right into his striking green eyes.

"But you have to see this for what it is," I shouted.

I heard the cheers stop. More a curiosity now, a sense of confusion.

I saw Adam frown.

"Adam isn't looking out for you. Adam's sole priority is getting my powers. Taking them from me so he can rule. He's pretending he believes in you by giving you powers. But if that's true, then why has he stopped? Why has he changed his goal to turning on the First Wave? Why has he changed from peace to war?"

There was a mixed response from the crowd then. Like some of them were infuriated by what I was saying, but at the same time, some of them were curious.

"Stop this trash," Adam said. "He's manipulated you before," he called. "Don't let him manipulate you ag—"

"Remember what happened the last time you followed something that seemed too good to be true? The ULTRAbot program? Remember how that turned out?"

More of a muffled response. People turning to one another, like they were awakening from a haze.

"It turned out to be Saint. And I'm telling you, right here, that this guy is no god. He's Saint 2. Well. I would say that, if he weren't such an insult to Saint's powers."

I saw Adam blush. Saw the anger building up inside.

"This isn't your hero. This is just another conqueror. And when he's done with you, he'll toss you aside. Just like he has Damon here."

I wasn't sure how the crowd reacted to that. I wanted to stay here and try and reach out for them for longer.

But by Adam's side, I saw people emerge. Adam's followers. Lots of them.

All of them floating past Adam.

Coming toward me.

"And now look what he does to people who stand against him," I said. "Look how weak your god is now. He can't even fight."

Adam, who was at the other side of a crowd of his charged-up ULTRAs, smiled now.

"Is that so?" he asked.

He walked up to Cassie.

Pressed a hand against her head.

I flew at him. But before I could get anywhere, I felt a pain shoot through my side, another damned electrical bolt, and I fell to the roof.

"I can't fight, huh?" Adam asked, as he pressed down further against her head.

I saw the tears in her eyes. I heard the pain in her voice. I tried to move, to shake free of the clutch of the anti-energy, but I couldn't.

"Let's see about that," Adam said.

He pushed harder against Cassie's head.

I saw smoke.

Heard a bang, then a flash of light.

Cassie dropped to the roof, eyes closed.

There was total silence, then. At least it felt like that. I knew Dad was crying out. I knew there was commotion.

But all I saw was my sister lying there just as she had all those years ago.

Lying there, motionless, all over again, with smoke forming around her.

Adam stepped over her. He walked right up to me. He lifted my chin.

"Anything to say?"

I gritted my teeth. Blasted free of the anti-energy charge that'd repressed me, as pain and fear filled my body.

Then I felt ice spread across my hands, then my entire body.

"Give up," I said. "I'll give you three chances. No more."

Adam smiled. "Good," he said, ignoring my command. "I didn't think so."

He tightened his fists.

Purple electricity—just like the kind that used to cover Cassie's hands—sprouted from his palms.

Then he pulled back a fist and cracked it into my face.

49

I felt Adam's fist crack across my face, and I knew the time to take a stand for humanity was now.

I dug my heels in as the rain lashed down from the thick clouds above. I felt myself flying backward, as a swarm of Adam's followers surrounded me. There were lots of them now. Thirty. Forty. Maybe more. And behind them, Damon, Avi, Ellicia, Cassie, Dad.

I couldn't let them get too far out of sight.

I couldn't let anything happen to them.

I took a punch from an ULTRA with rocks for hands, a little like Stone. I grabbed the rock, twisted the ULTRA around, then threw him at the crowd running at me. Above, I saw movement, and realized a flying ULTRA was powering down at me.

I dodged it, slipping a little in the process.

Then when I regained my footing, I fired ice at that ULTRA.

A lot of ice.

I looked around at the crowd of ULTRAs and I saw then exactly what I could do. I could freeze them all. I didn't necessarily have to kill them, just freeze them while I dealt with

Adam. And sure, it wouldn't go down well with the people. They'd probably see me as even more of a villain.

But if that's what it took to protect their best interests, even if they hated me for it, it's what I had to do.

I lifted my hands and felt the pressure building behind my palms. Every hair on my body stood on end as I scanned the crowd. I didn't have enough time to create a wormhole. The ice would have to do. It'd have to suffice, for now—

Then I felt someone smack my shoulder and I fell to my knees.

I felt an agonizing pain rip through my body, like my insides were being sucked out through a straw. It was only when I looked up that I saw Adam standing over me, and he had that glove pressed against me.

He smiled. I saw tingling light creeping up his arm. "You didn't have to take the hard route," he said. "And you still don't."

I gritted my teeth as my powers simultaneously got stronger and weaker. It was as if my body was fighting some kind of invading vaccination, trying desperately to kick the sickness out while at the same time soaking it up for its own benefit.

I saw Cassie, still paralyzed, with everyone else I loved beside her.

I knew that if I didn't act fast, I'd reach that state too.

"Neither do you," I said. "Give up. While you still have the chance."

Adam smiled. He shook his head again. He clearly wasn't giving in anytime soon. "You just don't get it, do you?"

I shrugged. "Neither do you."

I closed my eyes.

I'd be back for my family. I'd be back for my friends. I'd be back for my girlfriend.

But right now, I had somewhere to be.

I grabbed Adam's shin and teleported the pair of us far away.

We appeared in the middle of the desert somewhere. The heat was stifling.

But Adam was still holding on to my shoulder. His glove was ripping my powers from my body.

I punched at his legs, knocking him over.

When he was on his back, I stood over him, tightened my telekinetic grip around his neck, and pulled him upright.

"I'll tell you what the hard route is," I said, venom in my voice. "The hard route is continuing to fight. I don't want to have to kill you. But if I have to, to save the people from you..."

Adam smiled. "What?" he spluttered. "You'll kill me, will you? Bullshit. You won't kill anyone. Not when we're your own kind."

"You're not my own kind."

Adam laughed. "Oh, really?"

Then he snapped my telekinetic grip and slammed into my chest.

I flew back into the sand. I could feel him getting tougher, using up Cassie's powers.

"If you keep fighting, you'll have those powers to keep," I said. "You'll never get my powers."

Adam wrapped his hands around my neck. He tightened them harder than he'd ever done before. "Maybe I don't need them."

I tried to kick back. I tried to activate my powers. But the more I struggled, the weaker I got.

He was using Cassie's powers.

He was giving up on mine and he didn't even need mine.

He was defeating me.

"You'll... you can have mine. But not hers. Never hers."

I grabbed the sides of his head and with the last ounce of energy in my body, I teleported us back to New York.

We landed right on the rooftop of that Staten Island building. My vision was blurred, because Adam still had his grip around my neck. But in my blurred vision, I saw things that made me feel better about everything. I saw Stone fighting back. I saw Vortex and Ember too, all battling above me with Adam's followers.

They'd believed in me. After all this time, they'd believed in me.

Maybe I wouldn't make it, but they'd believed in me. That was the main thing.

I felt myself getting weaker as Adam's grip got tighter. He leaned right down, moved close to my face.

"This is a new age now, Kyle. An age that doesn't require you. Not anymore."

"My powers," I said. My voice was raspy. I could hardly speak. "Not hers. Not... not hers."

I started to panic even more. Because I needed him to take my powers away if my plan was to work. I couldn't have him give up on my abilities, killing me and keeping Cassie's powers in the process. That wasn't part of the plan.

Adam smiled, like he was enjoying the power he had over me.

Then, he said: "You know, I think I'll take you up on that offer."

He let go of his grip around my neck.

He put a hand on my chest and started to suck my powers away.

As agonizing as it was for me, as painful as it was to face, Adam didn't realize he'd just made the biggest mistake of his so-called reign.

50

I felt Adam ripping my powers from my body and I knew it was almost time.

I was on my back on the roof of that Staten Island building, but in truth I could've been anywhere. The clouds above were parting, and I could see a bright light burning through them. I wasn't sure whether it was the sun, or just my powers being lifted above me, into Adam's body.

In all truth, I was surprised he'd fallen so deeply into my trap.

The trap of bringing him back here.

The trap of offering my powers to him on a plate. An offer that I knew he would find extremely difficult to resist.

But even so, the hard part of what I had to do was far from done.

I just had to wait for the perfect moment.

I saw the explosions of the conflict above me and I wished things had never come to this. I saw what it represented. *My kind* versus *humankind*. And I was ashamed. Ashamed that things had got to a point where we seemed so disconnected from the people that they actually were willing to rise up against us.

We had work to do. I saw that now.

But in the back of my mind, as Adam pulled my powers away even harder, and the prospect of a powerless life dawned on me all over again, I saw the looks of fear I'd seen on the streets below. I saw that glimmer of hope in the eyes of people who had lost everything because of my recklessness and ULTRAkinds' recklessness. I saw it, and I knew that we could fix it. I absolutely knew it.

I reached for Adam's ankle, stretching out as slowly as I possibly could. I had to be ready for my moment. If I survived long enough for my moment.

I felt the powers being pulled even harder from me. I saw the fighting overhead. I saw the Resistance—what was left of it— trying to reach me and save me.

But I didn't want them to save me.

Because if they saved me, I couldn't complete my plan.

The pain of my powers was getting intense. I knew that if my focus slipped, even just for a split second, that I would lose my grip on the world. I smiled when I thought about what Damon had said to me on that Iceland trip. "Have you ever been to space?"

Well I had now.

And I had no intentions of visiting again.

Someone else, on the other hand...

Adam leaned right into my ear. I was weak now. Holding on to the last ounce of my powers. "Any last words?"

I laughed. I couldn't control it. I couldn't resist. I just burst out laughing hysterically, as the chaos and the destruction unfolded all around.

Adam frowned. For a split second, he actually looked concerned. "What? What's so funny?"

I kept on laughing.

"What's so funny?" he roared.

I felt the last bit of my powers—the last thing I was holding on to—being ripped away.

I felt Adam loosening his grip. Felt his body softening. Felt his guard dropping.

"Check your ankle," I said.

He frowned even further. "What—"

"My powers might be strong, but I've learned to master them. I've worked hard on reeling them in. It's kind of like riding a bike, or something. Sure, the bike might be powerful as hell. But if you don't know how to ride it..."

Adam kept on looking down at his ankle. I knew right then that he could feel what was there, but couldn't see it. "What're you on about?"

"My powers," I said. "They were the only thing keeping you rooted to the planet."

"How—"

"And now you've taken them from me, well. There's nothing I can do to stop the next part. Enjoy Jupiter, Adam. I hear it's fiery."

His eyes widened.

I saw his leg shake, as the invisible rope-like wormhole I'd wrapped around it—the wormhole that was connected intrinsically to my own abilities—finally gave way.

His hands covered in ice. He flashed in and out of invisibility. He lifted his arms to fire at me.

"Damn you—"

Then the rope-like wormhole dragged him from the surface of the earth and pulled him out of the sky.

One second, he was there.

The next, he was gone.

I leaned back against the earth. My eyes were sore. I wasn't sure whether the fighting was still going on around me, just that I was weak. So weak.

I smiled as I pictured Adam floating through space toward certain death. Maybe he'd master my powers in time to save himself. I doubted it, though. Really doubted it.

I thought back to the moment I'd put the cogs of my own demise in motion. I'd looked down into Krakatoa, and I'd created a wormhole that led all the way into Jupiter, all the way into deep space. I'd turned that wormhole into a narrow, lengthy invisible rope with my abilities, and hooked it to the core of Jupiter as well as I could.

And then I tied myself to that wormhole.

I made sure the only thing that could stop me being sucked away into it were my own abilities. I'd made sure they were totally linked, immersing myself inside that wormhole, risking everything to make it as dangerous as it was.

I knew that eventually, I'd lose my grip, and that wormhole would pull me away toward Jupiter, if I didn't defeat Adam.

And I knew the best way to defeat Adam was to give up my abilities to him. Because he'd wanted them so badly.

After creating the rope-like wormhole, I'd gone back to New York.

I'd given Adam a chance. A chance to give up. A chance to accept that he couldn't go on with his false leadership.

But when he took Cassie's abilities away, I knew there was no turning back then.

There was only one place Adam was going, and I had to make sure it happened.

He'd seen my powers and they'd been too much to resist.

He'd taken them from me.

And the second he'd taken them from me, I wasn't pulling back against the suffocating mass of the invisible, rope-like wormhole anymore.

No one was. Because Adam didn't know how to yet.

Adam had killed himself.

I tasted bitterness in my mouth at the thought of what I'd actually done. I'd killed Adam. He wasn't one of our own, not really. But killing anyone was against our code.

Well, things had changed.

I'd taken responsibility.

And I'd given up my abilities in the process.

I took a deep breath of the cool breezy air and felt specks of rain hit my face.

I pictured my family. Dad. Cassie. Daniel. And Mom.

And I pictured Damon and Avi. I pictured us putting everything behind us, moving on.

Then I pictured Ellicia.

I smiled when I thought of Ellicia. I hoped that one day, now my powers were gone, we could get back to normal. *Really* get back to normal.

But for now, all I wanted was sleep.

Darkness surrounded me.

A warm comforting blanket covered me.

I heard a voice—my mother's voice—telling me everything was going to be okay.

And then I slept.

51

I didn't expect to open my eyes again.

When I opened them, I was still on that Staten Island rooftop. Only this time, I wasn't surrounded by conflict.

I was surrounded by people, ULTRAs, everyone, all looking down at me with faces of concern. All of them checking I was okay.

"Is he alive?"

"I swear I saw him open his eyes then."

"Goddammit," Stone grumbled. "None of you ever trained in waking someone up before?"

He grabbed the sides of my body.

"Kyle! Are you with us? Are you—"

"Yes," I gasped.

Everyone went totally silent then. All of the whispers, all of the speculation, all of it stopped.

I heard a collective sigh of relief, and I knew right then I'd won the people back.

"Kyle," Ellicia said. She appeared at my side, almost out of nowhere. "Come on. Let's get you to your feet. Let's get you to a hospital or something."

I struggled to my feet. I felt so weak. I wasn't sure if this was just what it used to feel like, before I'd uncovered my powers. I wasn't sure whether this was just normality, and I'd been living an abnormal life for so long.

Whatever it was, I was just relieved that I was alive.

And not only me.

Cassie, too.

She was sat at the edge of the rooftop. She looked weak, like she'd been fighting the same inner and outer struggles as I had.

But she was still here.

That was the main thing.

I half-smiled. Nodded.

She gazed back at me, and nodded back in turn.

When I looked around, smiling at Dad, Avi, and even Damon, I noticed the crowd of ULTRAs—newly turned ULTRAs—weren't fighting anymore.

Some of them were totally pale. Some of them looked sick. Some of them were crying, like the reality of what they'd been doing, of the horrible ways they'd been fighting against the Resistance put in place to protect them, was finally dawning on them.

"I'm sorry," one of them, a bald man in a Captain America T-shirt said. "I just—I just thought it was the right way. I just thought it was the right goddammed way."

It was hard to feel any kind of pity for the man. After all, he'd been one of the people who'd fought against me and tried to put an end to the rest of the Resistance. He'd fallen for Adam's lies, and for that, he was foolish.

But at the same time, I knew that the uprising against me and the Resistance wasn't without legitimacy. People were worried. They were worried about a transition into a new world where they didn't really elect their leaders, and where global policy was decided by a privileged few who had the strength to crush them if they disagreed. Adam had struck a populist nerve. He'd made the people really believe they could be just as powerful as their newly elected leaders.

Of course, he'd been doing it all for self-gain. He'd been doing it for his own personal gain. He wanted to rule, and he saw that it'd be easy to justify rule if he won the people over to his way of thinking by handing out powers.

But since he'd been gone—and I hoped he really, really was gone now, as grim as a thing as that was to accept—I knew the people were seeing the truth all over again.

And I knew for a fact that I had to see the truth, too.

If I wanted to be respected, I had to be responsible. I had to listen.

I had to change.

We all did.

"I realize I haven't been the leader you want me to be," I said. "And I'm sorry I haven't heard you. I'm sorry for the people you might've lost. I'm sorry for... for making you feel like you were less than me and the Resistance, somehow. But that's over now. Those times are gone. And we're gonna have to work together if we want to move forward. It isn't gonna be easy. Not now thousands more people around the globe have powers, which means the potential for thousands to go rogue. But I don't want to think about the negatives. I've had enough of the negatives. If we work together, all of us... if we listen to each other, then we can make this work. I really believe that."

Silence followed my words. Total silence in the streets. Total silence from the crowd around me.

I waited for the applause. For the rapturous acceptance that I was back, and that I now had everyone's best interests at heart.

I didn't get that applause.

There was, however, a muted acceptance. A general feeling that this was how things were going to be. That we were going to have to move forward if we didn't want to destroy ourselves. Because we'd come so close, now. We'd come so close to self-destruction so many times. We couldn't come that close again. Ever again.

I felt an arm behind my back when I looked down at the crowds below.

It was Dad.

He smiled at me, patted my back in that way he always did when he was proud.

Then Ellicia stepped to my other side. After her, Avi. Cassie. Stone. Ember. Vortex.

Then Damon.

I looked at Damon. I wasn't sure how to feel about him. I wasn't sure I'd totally forgiven him.

But then I remembered my own words and I knew I couldn't afford to hold any hate towards him. Not anymore.

I nodded at him.

With a little hesitation, he nodded back.

Then, together, we looked out at the streets, out at the people below us, all of us—my ULTRAs and people, Adam's followers, and all of us were together.

I looked up at the sky. If I squinted enough, I could see a speck. I smiled as I pictured Adam trying to use the powers he'd so desperately wanted to break free of his inevitable fate.

It wasn't the old way of doing things. It wasn't Orion's way of defeating an enemy. It wasn't code.

But it was a new world. And what was done had to be done.

I'd taken responsibility.

I'd paid the price for it.

Now, I lived with it.

My family by my side.
My friends by my side.
My girlfriend by my side.
My people by my side.

52

A dam saw the bright light of Jupiter surging toward him and he held his breath.

He didn't have to hold his breath. He could breathe in space, of course. That's what Kyle's powers had given him the ability to do. Sure, he was rusty. The powers would take some time to master.

But he was going to master them.

He was going to survive this.

If he could just shake that tie from his torso...

He focused on his stomach. He focused on trying to release himself from that grip. Damn Glacies. Damn him for this. Just when he thought he'd seen his moment for ruling opening up right in front of him, he'd denied him that opportunity once again.

He thought he was one step ahead of him. So long, he'd acted like he was cleverer than him. Like he had the upper hand.

Well Adam was going to prove him wrong. He was going to show him *exactly* who had the upper hand.

Just had to get this tie from his body...

He looked back, his body covered in ice, and he saw Earth. It looked beautiful from this distance. So beautiful that it brought a tear to his eye. Even if he didn't survive, at least he had that. He'd achieved so much. He'd come so far to be at this point. He didn't want it to be over. Not yet. There was so much more to see. So much more to achieve.

And then he spun around and saw the surface of Jupiter edging ever nearer.

The light was so bright that it burned away his vision in an instant. He could feel the planet's gravitational pull dragging him towards it. He struggled more with that tie around his body, as his acceleration increased.

For a split second, just a split panicked second, he heard a voice in his head.

And the voice spoke words that terrified him.

"Was it all worth it?"

When he opened his eyes and saw the fires and molten lava of Jupiter just meters away, for the very first time, he wasn't sure if it was.

He went to scream.

He didn't get the chance.

The tie around his body finally came loose.

But there was nothing left of Adam to fight back.

53

I knew Damon and I were going to have to have this conversation at some stage.

The sun was out in full force in New York. It was roasting and stuffy. I was sweaty as hell, so I dreaded to think how Damon must be getting on, being bulkier than me.

We were in the shade of my dad's mechanics now. The place I'd first trained myself when I discovered my abilities. It hadn't changed much in the last year. Dad came here a lot more often, though, so it was much tidier, less dusty. There was that nice smell of oil about the place, which reminded me of childhood, riding in the back of his car. In those memories, it seemed like Cassie was there. But that was after her "death". And the more I focused on those memories, the more I remembered other little details. Like the tear in Mom's eye. And the empty look on Dad's face.

The kind of subtleties you pretend not to notice, which are too hurtful to process.

The kind of memories you hope time buries and glosses up, replacing it with perfection.

Sitting opposite Damon was kind of like that right now.

He was slumped over. He'd lost weight, in his defense. He hadn't looked me in the eye in a long time. Three days had passed since I'd cast Adam off the face of the earth and seen in the dawn of a new era. An era where ULTRAs were much more of the norm. Where The Resistance couldn't just be a single body in itself, but had to stretch its wings to span the globe. Where the world had to take responsibility for itself.

And where I was powerless.

Or at least, that's what people thought.

"Hear there's a new milkshake place," Damon said.

I wanted to smile at the normality of his words. He was obsessed with milkshake places. I was pretty confident there wasn't another of those stores out. It was kind of his go-to thing to say whenever he was uncomfortable.

"Damon."

He shrugged.

"Damon, look at me."

Damon lifted his head. For a moment, his eyes met mine.

Then he looked right away again.

"What happened. Between us. It's done."

"But it's not done," Damon said. His voice broke. He lifted his hands. I saw the powers tingling at his skin. "Not as long as I have these."

I walked over to him. Put a hand on his back. It was hard for me to do, especially to a best friend who I thought I trusted, and who I thought trusted me. But I knew it was the right thing to do. "I was annoyed with you. No doubt about that. I think it was a snake-ish thing to do."

"I never wanted to be a snake."

"Well you were. But what's done's done. And weirdly, I guess you made me realize a few things. Like the mistakes I'd made. And if you hadn't stood against me then... hell. Maybe I would never have realized."

Damon didn't respond to that. There was silence between us. "I betrayed you."

"You were worried about me and you were worried about what was happening to people. I get that. And I'm sorry if I ever made you feel anything other than a best friend."

"I... I killed Daniel."

A bitter taste filled my lips. I remembered watching Daniel take the full force of Damon's powers. Then not long after that paralyzing blow, I'd watched as one of Adam's followers eliminated him completely. "You didn't kill Daniel," I said. "Adam killed Daniel."

"But I—"

"You were just doing what you thought was the right thing. Daniel got caught up in it. I... I forgive you."

Damon leaned into me then. He rested his head on my shoulder.

"Hey, now," I said. "Not too close."

He sniggered a bit, sniveling in the process. "Right."

"Don't want any rumors going round."

"Sure," he laughed. "Sure."

It was weird seeing Damon so broken down. So out of jokes. He usually had a joke for everything.

I was confident those jokes would return, someday. But it would take time. The wall that'd been formed between us wouldn't rebuild itself overnight. He was right. He had betrayed me. But I'd betrayed him too.

The reparations were a two-way thing.

"As for your powers," I said.

When I pulled the glove from behind my back, I saw the shock on Damon's face. "How did you—"

"There's more than one of these gloves in circulation. Well, two, and if Psycho Adam found one, I was pretty determined to get my hands on the other. But anyway. What I want to know is, do you really want to give up your powers? 'Cause I can take them from you. Right now. If that's what you want."

Damon looked at the glove, then back at me. He was like a kid in a sweetshop.

I saw that red electricity bolt down his arms.

Then I saw him glance at the glove.

"I think I'll hold onto them. Just for a short while."

I half-smiled. Lowered the glove. "Good. We can have some fun with Avi now."

Out of nowhere, Damon grabbed me and hugged me.

"I'm sorry," he cried.

I rested my hands on his back and patted it. "Don't be."

"I just—I... I'm so sorry."

I closed my eyes when I felt myself tearing up. And I let myself hold onto my best friend of so many years too. "Me too," I said. "Me too."

We sat there in my dad's mechanics for a long, long time, not saying a single word, just holding onto one another and crying.

When it felt like enough time had passed before our holding and crying got weird, I pulled myself from Damon's bear hug and headed over to the door of the mechanics.

"Where will you go?" Damon asked.

I turned around and frowned. "What d'you mean?"

"Now your powers are gone. Where will you go?"

Now your powers are gone. Hearing Damon say those words made me realize just how much I was deceiving people all over again. But they couldn't know the truth. Part of my "sacrifice" for the "greater good" was that I'd given up my powers in the name of the people.

And sure. I had given them up.

But already I could feel those powers building inside me again.

And nobody could find that out. Ever.

"I guess I'll just go back to my old life," I said.

"Being a wussy nerd?"

I smiled. "Something like that. Goodbye, Damon."

"'Goodbye, Damon'? What is this, some kind of cliched action movie?"

I found myself laughing at Damon freely then. Damon laughed too, in turn. "I knew I'd never lose you," I said. "Not really."

Damon's smile turned. It turned just enough for me to understand that he didn't feel the same. He'd worried he'd lost me. And he still worried he'd lose me. "Stay safe," he said.

I nodded.

Then I turned around and walked out into the humid summer air.

54

I stood at the top of the Empire State Building, invisibility activated, and waited for my sister to appear.

Got to admit, standing at the top of the Empire State Building was a nervy feat in itself, invisible or not. I was getting there in terms of my abilities. I felt a lot more recharged. Not as strong as I had been once upon a time, perhaps. But stronger than when Adam had taken my powers away for sure.

Still, I worried about being here. Nobody knew I had my abilities.

Well. Just one person knew I had my abilities.

Cassie.

I looked across the bustling city of New York. I could see Staten Island in the distance, the place I'd called home all my life. Down below, I heard horns and the buzz of traffic. I could smell the fumes from the fast food restaurants and the street vendors and the exhaust fumes. But that wasn't a bad thing. This was New York. This was home.

I looked at the sun half-set and I realized she should be here by now. I'd told her she was strong. That she could find it in herself to rediscover her abilities. I'd managed to recharge, even after Adam had taken my abilities away. So I knew Cassie would be able to, too.

She told me she didn't think so. She told me she didn't think she was as strong as me.

I told her she was wrong about that. Totally wrong.

I was about to turn away when I saw movement whooshing below.

For a second, I thought it was Cassie. But I soon realized they were just humans. Well, humans with ULTRA abilities now. Former followers of Adam.

They would be a problem. While they seemed happy enough for now, I knew there was an even greater chance of ULTRAs going rogue and fighting back. The Resistance had collapsed, perhaps in its time of greatest need.

But I saw why the Resistance had failed. People didn't like bodies being created above them. They didn't want to feel like they were being trodden down into the dirt, or less important now for whatever reason.

That was why I had to keep a low profile.

Not just because I knew humanity would struggle with the idea that the ULTRA with the greatest abilities was still amongst them, and still powered.

But also because I needed to watch over them from the shadows.

As a great story once said, I might not be the hero these people wanted. But I was the hero they needed.

It was then that I saw her.

She was just a dot against the sun. She was only there for a split second, so she wouldn't catch the eye of anyone else.

But I saw her.

And when I saw her, I knew.

She disappeared almost as quickly as she'd appeared.

But she didn't have to be present any longer.

Cassie had her abilities back.

I had my abilities back.

Together, we would look out for this world, behind the scenes.

I looked up at the clouds. Wherever Orion and Daniel were, I hoped they were proud of us. I hoped we were making the right call.

I looked back down at the streets of New York. In an alley-way, I saw someone hold a gun to a woman's head, another man snatching her handbag away.

I took a deep breath and made my invisibility stronger.

I clenched my fists, and felt ice stretch up my arms.

Then I jumped off the Empire State Building and into the next world.

55

When Daniel Septer opened his eyes, he had no recollection of why he was in so much pain.

His body was on fire. Completely on fire. He tried to look around, but all he saw was darkness. He felt like he was floating, and as much as that intense heat suffocated him, part of him wondered whether he even had a body at all.

Then he saw a light.

It was in the distance. And something about that light made him want to go towards it. The closer he got to it, the more his memories came back.

He'd been fighting.

He'd been fighting with Kyle.

And then he'd been captured.

And then...

A sickness filled his mouth. As he looked around this vast, empty darkness, he knew where he was. He was in some kind of wormhole. Of his own making? Of Kyle's making? He wasn't sure. Perhaps some kind of safety mechanism had kicked in right before his powers had been stripped away.

Something had happened. He wasn't sure what.

All he cared about was getting to that light.

He pushed even further. The burning on his body intensified, but he grew more comfortable and accepting of it.

As the light got closer, he realized it wasn't a light at all.

It was a...

He narrowed his eyes.

His jaw dropped.

"Don't look so surprised," the voice said.

Daniel didn't know what to say. He didn't know what to think. "But—"

"You really think I was gone for good? Don't be so naive. Now come on. We've got to discuss the next step."

"The next step?" Daniel was transfixed, his consciousness failing to accept or understand that this person could still be alive. "What... what next step?"

The man opposite drifted further into the light.

The bottom half of his scarred face illuminated, and he smiled.

"Getting out of this place. And getting back to Earth. Together."

WANT MORE FROM MATT BLAKE?

The fifth book in The Last Hero series, Era of the ULTRAs, is now available to purchase.

If you want to be notified when Matt Blake's next novel in The Last Hero series is released, please sign up for the mailing list by going to: http://mattblakeauthor.com/newsletter Your email address will never be shared and you can unsubscribe at any time.

Word-of-mouth and reviews are crucial to any author's success. If you enjoyed this book, please leave a review. Even just a couple of lines sharing your thoughts on the story would be a fantastic help for other readers.

mattblakeauthor.com
mattblake@mattblakeauthor.com

Made in the USA
Coppell, TX
25 September 2021